Seasons of Love: Book Five

It's a Summer Thing

Four Summer Themed Romances to Get your Beach Read on . . .

By

LORI LEGER
KELLIE KAMRYN
KAREN SUE BURNS
CARMINE VALENTINE

Seasons of Love: Book Five
It's A Summer Thing
Compiled and arranged by:

 CAJUNFLAIR
PUBLISHING

ISBN-10:1940305071
ISBN-13:978-1-940305-07-3

ACKNOWLEDGMENTS

Cover art and interior formatting by
Lori Leger/Cajunflair Publishing
http://www.CajunflairPublishing.com

Edited by Karen Sue Burns and Lori Leger

TABLE OF CONTENTS

FULL CIRCLE SUMMER
By
Lori Leger

3:33 A.M. – March 4th – Lake Erin
A small town in southwest Louisiana

Come back to me, Cat . . .

Cathryn McDaniel Ferguson woke from the dream, her face wet with tears, her soul heavy with sadness. Her gaze settled on the time being projected onto her bedroom ceiling from the alarm clock. A single sob tore through her before she could stop it. In seconds Zachary was upright, his hand on her shoulder and his voice filled with quiet concern.

"Cathryn? Are you all right?"

She clutched her husband's hand, and pushed back another fast-approaching sob. *Just a dream.* "I-it-it was just a dream." *Or a nightmare.*

"Again? Oh babe, come here. Let me hold you. She pushed at his hands. "I have to pee first." She swung her legs off of the bed, trying to find her slippers.

His low chuckle came from somewhere in the darkness behind her. "Of course you do."

"What's your point?" She shuffled to the bathroom, still walking somewhat normally for a woman five months pregnant for twins.

"None . . . no point . . . none at all."

She grinned as she emptied her bladder for the first time that day. Only the first of many times. By the time she reached the bed, Zach had the covers pulled back for her.

"Come on over here, Cat. Let me warm you up." He hissed like a snake when her icy hands hit his warm abs, chiseled from two decades of hard work.

"Sorry, water was ice cold when I washed my hands."

He grunted. "S'okay, you're worth it."

"Aw, you say the sweetest things."

"I have to lately, or else," he mumbled.

"What?"

"Nothing, babe. Go back to sleep."

She let it go, knowing good and damn well he was right. "I can't, or I don't want to."

"Tell me about the dream."

"I'd rather not." She sensed the lift of his head off his pillow.

"That bad?"

She squeezed her eyes shut, trying to block out the memory of fighting to come back from something, or someplace . . . she didn't know what or where. He pulled her closer and she curled into him, searching for the solace she found only in this man's presence.

"Zach?"

"Hmm?"

She paused, searching for words to express her feelings. "Can you believe this is our life? I mean, a year and a half ago, I was getting ready to marry another man."

"Until you realized he wasn't me."

She smiled. "No he wasn't."

"I know what you mean, though. It seems like we've had a lifetime of experiences just since you came back from Dallas. You realizing you couldn't live without me—"

"And then waking from a coma and thinking I still loved Christian."

He groaned. "Yeah, but luckily you got your senses back, and married the real man of your dreams."

Dreams. Her chest tightened with an unsettling feeling.

"Don't forget all that tedious, back-breaking effort we put into conceiving a child—"

Cat smiled in the darkness of their bedroom. "Ugh, I know, right? That was torture."

"—only to discover we conceived two." He nuzzled her neck. "We are such over achievers." He kissed the top of her head when she didn't answer.

"You sure you don't want to tell me about your dream?"

"I'm sure."

"But if it'll help to talk about . . ."

"I don't want to, Zach."

His large hand rubbed her back reassuringly. "Okay, babe."

Fear, deep and penetrating, rose from the pit of her stomach. She was afraid to talk about the dream, afraid to acknowledge it, to give it a face, a voice of its own.

All she could do was hope and pray it never manifested onto something more substantial than a dream.

May 5th – 31 weeks and 4 days into the pregnancy
Due date: July 4th (T minus 60 days and counting)

Cat Ferguson lay on her ob-gyn's examination table with her taut, pregnant belly rising above her like a great, beached whale.

"Are you sure you don't want to know the sex of your babies?"

She raised her head over the mound of belly, hoping her face showed her determination. "No! We want to be surprised—like in the old days."

Dr. Brown smiled, as he always did at her answer. "All righty, then." His silence as he read the remainder of the ultrasound report sent a chill of warning up Cat's spine.

"Everything okay, Doc? When you suck on your lower lip like that, it usually means you're about to give me a talking to. Blood pressure, sodium intake, feet swelling—you don't see a third baby inside there, do you?"

He grinned as he straightened and adjusted the collar of his white lab coat. "And that, young lady, is why I don't play poker." He placed his hands on her belly and felt around. "No way is there room for a third. But the ultrasound shows the placenta placement lower than I'd like to see it. Not unusual for twins, but by this time it's usually started to shift into a better position."

He reached inside a drawer and handed her two pamphlets with diagrams. "This is where your placenta should be, in the upper left quadrant. Yours was low lying before, but at an acceptable distance. I had hopes that it would migrate higher, most do. But it's migrated lower instead, to what we call a marginal placenta previa. It's a complication common with multiple births."

"What do you mean by migrate? Isn't the placenta attached to the uterus?"

"It's implanted, yes, but as the uterus expands and enlarges, the placenta grows toward the best blood supply in the upper quadrant. You're fortunate it's taken this long to get to this stage, normally it's 20 weeks."

"What does this mean for my babies?"

"It can lead to complications. If the placenta continues to drop, it might partially or completely cover the cervix, preventing the babies from entering the birth canal. Then you'd be looking at a Caesarean delivery to avoid a rupture."

"I want a natural delivery. Are you certain about this?"

He patted her hand. "Nothing's certain yet, Cathryn. But I want you to stay calm and take it easy the next two months. Don't stand, when you can sit. Don't sit when you have the opportunity to lie down, and put your feet up." He checked her chart again. "How's your water intake?"

"I'm drinking lots of water, and I've cut out all carbonated beverages. I'm also trying to stay away from sodium. If you knew how much I love eating boiled crawfish you'd know how difficult it's been for me to pass it up this entire season."

Her obstetrician's face pulled down in a distinct frown. "I had to give it up a couple of years ago, myself. I know exactly where you're coming from. If we're invited to a crawfish boil, I skip it. If I didn't, a team of wild horses couldn't drag me away from that table until I've eaten my fill."

Cat groaned. "Zach and I skipped another one this weekend."

"Good man, at least he's willing to skip them along with you. My wife tells me I'm on my own for a meal and goes anyway."

She couldn't stop the belly laugh from escaping. "Zachary wouldn't dare go to one without me. He'd be far too afraid of the consequences."

Doctor Brown released a low chuckle. "As well he should." He gave her belly a final gentle pat then helped her to an upright position. "I want to see you again in a week. Until then, if you start having any pains or bleeding, call me immediately. If it's heavy bleeding, get to the hospital right away. Oh, and I don't want you driving, either."

Cat closed her gaping mouth with a snap. "Seriously?"

"Absolutely. Driving can put a strain on that lower abdomen, believe it or not."

"How about sexual relations?"

"No."

"No restrictions?" she asked, hopefully.

"No sex. No stimulation. No orgasms . . . it could trigger contractions, could partially dislodge the placenta. It's a chain reaction." He shook his head. "Sorry—wish I had better news for you." He cocked his head to the side. "Do I need to get Zach in here to stress the importance of this? Some husbands think their wives are trying to get out of having sex."

"No need for that. Zach wouldn't do anything if it meant danger for these babies." She stifled a disappointed groan. It would take an intense effort to keep her hands off her husband. But these consequences were far too serious to ignore. "When— I mean—if I'd go into premature labor, would my babies be in any danger of . . ."

"They're totally viable with today's medical advances. Twins are usually slightly smaller, but from what I can tell from the ultrasound results, your babies are good size. They're already around 4 pounds each at this point. There may be some complications if the lungs aren't fully formed, but if you threaten premature labor, I'll suggest giving you a round of steroids to speed up the lung development. I doubt you'll carry to full term, anyway, but if you deliver two weeks early, which is about right for twins . . ." He twisted his mouth in concentration. "I'd say we're looking at babies somewhere in the five and a half to six pounds range. The longer before you go into labor, the better it is for your twins."

She nodded, determined to follow his orders to the tee. "I drove over here by myself. Should I call someone to pick me up?"

Doctor Brown gave his head an adamant shake. "I don't think that's necessary. Go ahead and drive home, but keep in mind it'll be your last time behind the wheel for a while."

May 15th – 33 weeks
T minus 50 days and counting

Zachary stood in front of the open freezer, checking out the offerings. "What do you feel like having for supper tonight, babe?"

Cat adjusted the pillow at her lower back, a constant source of pain for her. "What choices do we have?"

"Chicken, beef stew meat, pork sirloin roast, and chops. How about if I start up a beef stew in the slow cooker before I leave for the store?"

"That sounds excellent. Do we have any loaves of that frozen whole wheat bread left in there?"

Zach rummaged around in the freezer again. "I don't see any, but I'm sure your mom won't mind picking up a couple before she comes over this afternoon—especially if we invite both her and Doc Barton over for supper tonight."

"They love your beef stew."

"I know," he added, sending his wife a big grin. "That's because it's out of this flippin' world." Zach pulled the pack of lean stew mean out of the freezer and popped it into the microwave for a quick defrost. He leaned over the sofa to give his wife a kiss, and continued to collect the ingredients for his stew: Potatoes, carrots, onions, celery, bell pepper, parsley and various seasonings. By the time he'd defrosted and browned the stew meat, he had all the vegetables ready to add to the slow cooker. A few shakes of black pepper and a low sodium Cajun seasoning, along with one bottle of his secret ingredient, and the stew had reached the do-not-disturb stage in the slow cooking process. He covered the pot, adjusted the heat setting to low, and went to join Cat on the sofa.

He pulled her into his arms for a kiss, one that reminded him it'd been two weeks since he'd made love to his wife. He leaned forward to kiss her belly. Any sacrifice he made for the sake and safety of these two tiny lives, as well as the absolute love of his life, was totally worth it.

"God, I miss making love with you."

"Don't talk about it, Cat. It just makes it har— uh—more difficult. Let's keep the goal in sight. In a month and half, we'll have two healthy babies—two bouncing baby 'somethings' that are going to rob us of sleep for the next several months. That being said, I don't want you forgetting how important you are to me, and how much I adore you."

"I know you do. I feel it all day, every day. I love you so much, Zachary." She kissed him, a long and lingering kiss that had them both aching with need.

He pulled away, planting a last kiss on her nose. "I've got to go now, babe. I have a huge truckload due today, and I'll be busy as all hell unloading and organizing the rest of the afternoon." He rose from the couch and pulled his phone from his pocket. "I'll call your mom right now and ask her to pick up the frozen bread dough. You need anything before I go?"

"Nope. I'm fine." She smiled as she watched him leave. Her cat, Chableu, jumped up beside her on the couch, purring for attention. "Sit, boy. Mama needs to get some writing done today or my publisher is going to cancel my contract."

She managed to add another 1,000 words to her current Work In Progress, before her mother entered through the kitchen door.

"Hey, sweetie. How's my girl doing today?"

"I'm fine—we're all fine. I'm actually able to get some work done this morning."

"Is that the military novel you're working on?" Ellen lowered two bags of groceries onto the kitchen table.

"Uh huh—I'm working on the closing scene. I should have it cleaned up enough to send to my editor by Monday."

"Fabulous. And so are the smells coming out of that crock pot. What's that husband of yours got cooking up today?"

"His famous beef stew—and you and Pops are invited to supper. Didn't he tell you already?"

Ellen rummaged around in the pantry and came out with two loaf pans and the cooking spray. "He asked me to pick up this frozen bread dough. I'm putting it out to thaw and rise right now. Mmm . . . Gavin will be pleased. He and I both love Zachary's beef stew."

After a few minutes of puttering in the kitchen, Ellen sat next to her daughter. "I think I'll vacuum and mop your floors today."

"You don't have to do that, Mom. They're still clean from the last time. There's hardly any foot traffic in here."

"You obviously haven't been in the kitchen, lately."

"Not since Zach left this morning. Did he leave a mess? He was expecting a big delivery today and was kind of in a rush." Her mother's bland expression made her worry. "What?"

"It's—nothing. I'll just mop the kitchen floor."

"Stop. Pour yourself a cup of coffee and talk to me." She waited until her mom situated herself next to her on the couch.

Ellen set her coffee mug on the end table and reached out with both hands to cup Cat's significant belly. "How are my two babies? Maw Maw loves you both." She spoke to the mass of taught skin stretched over Cat's baby belly.

Cat considered her mom's previous behavior. "What's bothering you?"

Ellen waved off her question. "What? Nothing's bothering me. Why would you ask that?"

"You should know by now you can't hide anything from me. Now, spit it out."

"I just wish I knew when these babies were coming."

"Don't we all? Please tell me what's wrong."

Ellen's entire visage seemed to deflate before Cat's eyes. "Gavin surprised me with an Alaskan cruise package."

Cat gasped in delight. "You've always wanted to do that, Mom. Why are you so upset?"

"We'd have to fly out to Seattle in two days and we'd be gone for eleven days."

"That's great. You're always saying the best vacations are the ones that aren't planned, but happen spur of the moment."

"What if you go into labor while I'm gone?"

"I won't. I promise we'll wait for you and Pops to get back home."

"You can't make a promise like that, Cathryn. Those babies will come when they darn well want to."

"You're right, they will . . ."

"And I want to be here when they do."

"Mom—just go. Go, and have a wonderful time. It's not like you'll be completely out of touch with us. We'll talk daily and I'll let you know what's happening—every twinge, every single cramp."

"But—"

"No, call your husband right now and tell him you're going. Yes, I would like for you to be around when my babies are born, but if worse comes to worse, the only person I'll absolutely need is Zachary.

Trust me when I tell you, that man isn't going anywhere."

"Are you sure? The timing seems so . . . off, somehow."

Cat gave her mother an impatient huff and picked up her phone. She hit the first number on her speed dial list and waited. "Poppa Doc, this is Cat. Have you booked that flight to Seattle yet?"

"Yes, but your mom was so upset I'm considering rescheduling for the end of the season, in June."

"Don't you dare reschedule. Is the flight direct from Houston to Seattle?"

"We're catching a puddle jumper from Lake Coburn to Houston, then on to Seattle. It's so much more convenient to get our luggage checked in at the smaller airport."

"I agree. Don't change a thing. She'll be on it with you, I guarantee."

"Thanks, Cat. I've spoken to Doctor Brown and tried to reassure her, but she wasn't having any of it. I guess she had to hear it directly from you. I've had this flight and cruise booked since our wedding back in December."

Cathryn laughed at the angst in her step-dad's voice. "You're cutting it close but this is entirely doable. I'm determined nothing will happen with this pregnancy while you're on your trip."

Her step-dad chuckled over the phone. "I know exactly where you get that determination of yours— from your mother."

Cathryn smiled at Ellen. "I believe you're right. You two have loads of fun. Don't you let her spend one minute worrying about us—we'll be perfectly fine. I love you, Pops. And thanks for making one more of mom's dreams come true."

"Well—she makes mine come true every day we're together. I love you too, Cat."

She disconnected and used the phone to point at her mother. "Take lots of pictures and video, do you hear me? Honestly, I'm so jealous."

"Oh, Cat . . ." Ellen covered her face and burst into tears.

Cat hugged her close. "Stop, or you're going to make me cry, too." She yanked a tissue from the box on the end table and handed it to the woman beside her. "Here."

Ellen wiped her eyes and sniffled into the tissue. "It's just that sometimes I feel as though things are going so well in my life, it can't last. You know what I mean?"

Leveling a serious gaze on her mother, she straight out lied to her. "Not really."

Ellen lifted one hand and let it fall limply into her lap. "The last time I was this satisfied with my life, this happy with the way things were panning out . . ." Her voice, already warbled with tears, cracked as her speech faltered.

"Dad died, right?" Cat sucked up her own undeniable feelings of dread as her mother's face crumbled into a teary mess. She let her cry, thanking God for giving her some semblance of strength to help her mother through this. "Please tell me you aren't feeling guilty for being so happy with Doc Barton. Dad would want you to be happy."

"I don't know, maybe, but it's more than that. It's just . . . it scares me sometimes. I want you all to be safe and protected from all harm, and as happy as you can be."

"Nothing in life is guaranteed. We know that. But if there's one thing I've learned from you, it's that whatever is meant to happen in our lives, will happen. We have to believe that whatever happens, good or bad, we'll get through it. Our faith, our family, our friends will all join forces to make that happen. Allow yourself to be happy, Mom. Kellie and I are fine."

Ellen placed a hand on her daughter's cheek. "How'd you get so wise?"

"I learned from the best teacher ever—my beautiful mother." She pulled her close for a big hug. "Now I think you should go home. You've got some packing to do." She raised a hand to stop her mother's protests. "I don't need a thing. Zac takes care of everything before he leaves. Go. But you and Pop come back for supper for some beef stew."

Ellen nodded. "Okay, but if you need anything, I'm a phone call away."

Cathryn nodded and watched her mother leave through the door she'd recently come through.

Things are going so well in my life, it can't last.

She'd told her mom she didn't know that feeling, but God, did she ever. Every time she looked at herself in the mirror and Zach's reflection appeared beside her, she had that same feeling. Every time she felt her babies kick, press against her side, or on her bladder, she had the feeling. As though her world revolved around her husband and her babies, and if anything happened to any of them, she wouldn't survive.

She grabbed another tissue from the box, and sniffled into it before wiping her eyes. Hormones—raging, pregnant woman hormones were to blame for this. "Stop Cat. Just stop," she blubbered, as Chableu approached his mistress, clearly concerned and purring up a blue streak.

How many times had she lain in bed at night thinking those very same words her mother had dared to speak? Could things in her life possibly get too good? After all, what had she ever done to be this kind of happy? She placed her hands on her belly, one on each side. Pressed gently on what could be the head of one twin, and the bottom of the other. Could she keep them safely inside? Keep them in her womb long enough to avoid the dangers of this world? Dear God, she hoped so.

She crumbled suddenly, filled with a heaviness of heart—an acute sense of loss and loneliness. For her father, whose wife had to learn to live without him. For her children, as well as Kellie's, who would never know the love of the man who'd raised them with such warmth, and understanding—allowing them to grow into the strong, secure women they were today. Even though they had Mr. John, Zach's dad, and Pops, as she'd taken to calling Doc Barton, they'd never know her dad, and it hurt.

She hurt for Zach, who had to be feeling the loss of his own mother right now. She wondered if either of her children would have his mother's fair complexion or green eyes.

"Oh God, enough already," she scolded herself, even as she heard the telltale scuffle at the door.

"Are you talking to me, sis?"

She turned to see her sister standing in the doorway, infant carrier in one hand, Diana's chubby toddler hand in the other. Just as suddenly as it arrived, the heaviness lifted, like a dense fog that had no choice but dissipate in the presence of warmth and sunshine. Silently she thanked whoever was responsible for sending Kellie and her babies to brighten her day.

Diana chortled and walked toward her, taking several unsteady steps in Velcro strapped sandals decorated with sparkly daffodils. Cathryn had no choice but to smile. Because surely, sadness had no place in the presence of such joy.

Kellie set down the carrier and lifted her six week old son from the seat. "I think Auntie Cat has a case of the blues, kids. It looks like we got here just in the nick of time."

Cat accepted her nephew greedily and cradled him in her arms. "Girl, you have no idea."

May 22nd – 34 weeks
T minus 43 days and counting

Zach brought his wife a tall glass of iced raspberry tea. "Have you heard from your mom today?"

"Thanks sweetie." Cat took a sip. "Mmm, that's delicious." She picked up her phone and scrolled to the text her mother had sent her earlier, along with several shots of Alaska. "They took the Mendenhall Glacier tour today, did some whale watching, and then rode a train through Mendenhall Valley. She says it's every bit as beautiful and impressive as she'd always heard." She handed the phone to Zach and he flipped through the shots, whistling under his breath.

"That is really something. How about it, babe? You want to go to Alaska one day?"

Her nose wrinkled in distaste. "I'm sure it's a fabulous cruise, but I'd much prefer something more tropical, like Hawaii. I'll take the sand and sea any day over snow and glaciers." She patted her belly and gave a slightly hysterical snort. "And who needs to go to Alaska for whale watching when you can do it right here from the comfort of your own living room."

Zach placed her feet gently in his lap and began massaging them. "By the time we go, that baby bump will be long gone, and you'll look as good in a bikini as you ever did."

"Humph . . . the bump may be gone, but not forgotten."

"You know, if you ever decide to switch to a one piece, it won't hurt my feelings one little bit. I'd just as soon not have every man on the beach gawking at my gorgeous wife."

"I may not have a choice. By the time I'm done, I'll only be fit for one of those mu-mu's my great-grandma used to wear. Look at me, Zach. I'm huge."

"Just remember, Cat. The bigger you get, the more our babies will weigh. Personally, I hope you get even bigger. Anybody can look at you and tell your belly is all baby. Where are you going now?"

"I've got to go pee."

"You just went."

"I drank something since then. I have to go again."

"Let me carry you. You shouldn't be on your feet." He leaned over to lift her.

Cat pushed his hands away. "You are not carrying me to the bathroom. I have to move every now and then to keep my back from hurting."

He helped her up and walked her to the bathroom, and then back to the couch when she was done. "You know, babe, from behind you don't even look pregnant."

She gave an audible snort. "I find that hard to believe. I can practically feel my butt getting bigger."

Zach stood behind her, looped his arms around to encompass her—all of her—belly and all. "Cathryn Jade, you're always beautiful to me, but now, carrying our children—you're breathtaking." He lowered his face into the crook of her neck, and breathed her into him. "Don't you know that?"

She let her head fall back against his chest. "I guess I do now."

"Here, sit. I've got something for you."

"Oh, I love surprises!"

His heart swelled with love for his precious wife. "Yeah, I kind of already know that about you."

"Uh huh—like this Mother's Day gift I didn't expect." She touched the exquisite watch on her wrist. "But I adore it."

"I know you do, but I kept asking if there was anything you wanted specifically, and you kept saying—"

"I already have everything I wanted. And that's the truth."

Zach reached into his shirt pocket and pulled out a black velvet box with a hinged lid. "That may have been true at the time, but not once you've seen this." She opened the box slowly and gasped. Zach's heart nearly exploded with joy as his wife's eyes filled with tears.

"Oh my God, Zach, this is exquisite." She lifted the box to better observe the glimmering effect of the diamond in motion—a clustered circle pendant of diamonds with a center circular diamond that spun to and fro, always in motion and catching the light. "How did you know?"

"I saw you close down the site when I walked in on you the other day. So, I checked the history on your laptop."

Tears trailed down her cheeks as she gazed up at him. "You didn't have to do this, you know. I was just curious about them. It didn't mean I had to have it."

He gave her a shrug and reached for the box. "I can always return it."

She snatched it from his reach. "Not after you went through all that trouble to spy on my browsing history."

"It was a means to an end." He raised his hands and dropped them. "Guilty, as charged. I'm ready for my sentencing."

Cat pushed out her lower lip. "Poor you, I sentence you to life."

He frowned. "Where?"

She looped her arm around his neck and pulled him close for a kiss. "Right here with me, Zack-attack. Are you going to ask for a re-trial? Or maybe plan an appeal?"

He removed the pendant from its box. "Hm. A retrial? I think not. Maybe I could appeal, but only to your good nature. Be gentle with me."

"Oh, I'll have to be considering the circumstances. But you just wait until our sentence of celibacy is over. I can promise I'll be anything but gentle with you."

Zach's eyes rolled back in his head at the thought. "Oh. God. I can't wait."

May 29th – 35 weeks
T minus 36 days and counting

"Oh. My. God. Cat-astrophe has truly let herself go."

Cathryn stiffened at the heartless comment, knowing the speaker immediately.

"Cat . . . Girlfriend, *when* did you get so *huge*?"

Girlfriend? Jeri Young DeVillier? Since . . . never. Cat would have recognized that irritating nasal tone of her high school nemesis anywhere. She'd seen her in the store earlier, and pleaded with Zach to push the wheelchair he'd confiscated for their "outing" as far away from her as possible. She had no desire to face anyone wearing size three jeans. Particularly someone who'd claimed superiority over the rest of the human race throughout four years of high school. Hindsight being what it was, it hadn't helped that Jeri had spent most of that time throwing herself at Zach. Apparently, the woman still had the same high opinion of herself.

Cat had to wonder if she plowed down the woman with her wheelchair, would anyone really give a damn?

She retracted her claws, and pasted on a smile, so artificially sweet it made her teeth hurt. "Why, thanks so much for noticing, Jeri. Yes, it started approximately eight months ago with a little condition called pregnancy."

"Oh, you're *en famille* . . ." The pixie-haired blonde's mouth puckered in distaste. "I didn't realize."

"Sure you didn't."

"But sweetie, I've had children, two of them, and I never got *that* huge."

"Unless you popped them out at the same time, I'm not surprised. I'm having twins."

"Twins? Oh, well . . . yes, I guess you *could* use that as an excuse."

Heat emanated from Cat's face and ears. Her blood pressure had jumped through the roof.

"But twins are usually so small. Surely those two tiny little things aren't taking up that much room. I bet you'll be stuck with a good fifty pounds of extra baby weight."

"That'd be difficult since I've only gained twenty-nine pounds." *Twenty-nine and a half, but who's counting?*

The corners of Jeri's mouth pulled down in a frown. "Really? I guess I hadn't seen you since you moved back to town. You must have put on some weight since high school." Jeri clucked her tongue as she stared down at her. "Poor Zachary."

Cat felt her claws lengthening—itching to scratch Jeri's eyes right out of her uppity, snobbish little head. "You know what you could do to make my day?"

"What's that, honey? Call a tow truck to get you back into your car?"

"You could kiss my big ole pregnant a—"

"Excuse us!" Zach rounded the corner, just in time to keep from having to peel his pregnant wife off the pitiful excuse for a lady.

"Zachary, you're looking as handsome and fit as ever." Her voice lowered to conspiratorial whisper. "I'm glad one of you has had the decency to keep yourself up."

"Jeri," he nodded at the blonde. "How's that raging case of chlamydia? Did you ever get that cleared up?"

Cat's laughter came in the form of snorts, as her husband rolled her away from the encounter, leaving Jeri coughing and sputtering like an old car. She reached up to grab onto his arms. "Well done, babe!"

"I thought so."

"That was epic. Did you see the expression on that pointy little face of hers? I thought her eyes would pop right out of her skull." She looked up at her husband. "Did she really have chlamydia, or did you make that up in order to make your big, fat wife's day?"

"Rumor has it she got it from sleeping with some college kid a couple of years ago. By the way, I found the perfect rug for the nursery."

"And?"

"And you're not fat, just pregnant. I mean, there are two babies taking up lots of space in there." He laid his hand lovingly upon her abdomen.

"No kidding." She placed her hands on her lower back and made a feeble attempt to arch it, an impossible act while sitting in the chair. "I can't even stretch anymore."   She considered the ravages her formerly trim figure had undergone during this pregnancy—the waddle in her walk, when Zach allowed it and her exceptional girth. Would her body ever recover? She hadn't gained much weightl, but surely her bladder would never be the same. The organ in question sent a spasm, a not-so-subtle protest against the tiny feet, or elbows, or baby butts pressing against it. "Oh hell, I've got to pee, again."

"Restrooms are way over there." Zach pivoted her chair in the opposite direction, clear on the other side of the store.

"Of course they are." Cat spied the bright restroom sign and released a low groan as she remapped her inner navigational chart. Zach pushed the wheelchair and she used the signs along the way to mark their progress—like beacons along an airport landing strip. Fitting analogy, since she was nearly as big as a plane. STORAGE . . . CABINET

HARDWARE . . . FASTENERS . . . APPLIANCES .
. . and finally RESTROOMS, her source of relief. "I
think society should make it completely acceptable for
pregnant women to wear adult diapers. It would save
tons of footsteps, for those who are allowed to walk,
anyway."

Zach nodded. "And time. It would save lots of
time."

She didn't bother to answer her husband,
knowing she'd practically blackmailed him into taking
this little side excursion before her doctor's
appointment. He didn't want her on her feet any more
than she had to be, per doctor's instructions. He'd
begged her to bypass the trip, even offering to take
pictures of suitable rugs and text them to her. She'd
insisted on being there in person. So he'd loaded up
their borrowed wheelchair and indulged her.

She left him standing just outside the women's
restroom with the chair. Within seconds after relieving
herself she discovered they had a serious problem.

Cat exited the restroom, trying to remain calm. It
was one thing to have your water break in the Home
Depot, something she'd dreaded happening. It was
considerably worse to mildly hemorrhage in the DIY
section. She sat in the chair and cleared her throat.
"We've got to go, babe. Now." Whatever panic she'd
refused to give in to took up immediate residence on
her husband's face.

"What? Is it time? What's going on? Did your
water break?"

"I'm bleeding, Zach."

His face turned a pasty white. "How much?"

"I think we should go straight to the hospital."

He took two steps in the opposite direction, turned back around and pointed at her. "Sit! Stay! I'm going to get a wheelchair for you."

"Zachary!"

"What?"

"I'm already sitting in a wheelchair."

"Right." Zach rushed her to the car and lifted her easily into the front seat. Maybe not as easily as it would have been twenty-nine and a half pounds ago, but still easy enough for her macho husband.

She took the opportunity to place her hand on his face and give him a kiss. "I love you, but hurry."

"I love you too, babe. It'll be fine. I know it will."

The rapid, sharp clip of heels alerted Zach to his sister-in-law's approach. He met her immediately and gave her a hug. "Thanks for coming, Kel. I'm a freaking basket case here by myself."

"How is she? Have you heard anything yet?"

He shook his head. "There are three teams of doctors in with her now. I'm about to lose my mind waiting to hear something." He scratched distractedly at his five o'clock shadow. "I haven't scraped up enough nerve to call Ms. Ellen and Doc yet."

Kellie cringed and made a face. "Let's not attempt that until we talk to Dr. Brown." She pulled up the couple's flight itinerary on her phone and showed him. "They just docked in Seattle, Zach. They won't be flying out of there until 7:15 tomorrow morning, 9:15 our time. Their connecting flight from

Houston should land at the Lake Coburn airport around 4:00 p.m." She dropped her phone in her purse. "It's too late to attempt finding an earlier flight out of Seattle. Especially one with only an hour and a half connect time like the one they have."

She covered her face with both hands. "God, I hope Cat doesn't have these babies until they get back. Poor Pops won't be able to get mom to leave the house again."

Zach nodded. "Misplaced guilt is a terrible thing, and there won't be a damn thing we can do to stop her from blaming herself."

The sound of the door opening had the two of them bolting up as Cat's doctor exited her room.

"How is she? Is she going into labor?"

"Is my sister okay? Are the babies okay?"

Dr. Brown lifted his hands at the onslaught of questions. "She's not showing any signs of early labor. But I'm afraid there'll be no way around a Caesarean delivery."

"Now, as in today?" Zach felt a sudden rush of light headedness.

"No, no. The bleeding isn't bad enough to schedule an immediate section. I'd rather be fully prepared. Just in case, I'm calling the teams I've assembled for a meeting. They're all here today, so the timing is perfect. I've ordered a single course of steroids to speed the development of the infants' lungs. I'm going to suggest that we schedule her section no later than five days from now. That's barring any complications that would push up that delivery date."

"Complications?" Zach's stomach flipped at the word. Complications were never good.

"Her water breaking, contractions, further bleeding, or worse, a full blown case of hemorrhaging. I'd rather err on the side of caution and proceed with a schedule. That way, we'll be better prepared if we have to jump into immediate action."

Thoughts of his wife in any of those situations, especially the latter, had Zach's heart constricting with terror. His feelings of dread must have translated to his face.

Dr. Brown gave him a comforting pat on the arm. "Don't worry, daddy. We've got this covered."

Much relieved at the doctor's vote of confidence in his team, the tension ebbed from Zach's body. "Can I see her now?"

"Sure you can. You may have to give the nurses a couple more minutes to finish getting her set up, but then you both can see her. Try to keep her calm and you do the same."

The father-to-be paced at the door until he could barely stand it.

"Zach, go on in there," Kellie insisted. "I'll wait until the room clears to go in. You need a minute alone with her."

He nodded, and entered the room, standing by until the occupants finished up their business with his wife.

Cat caught his eye and smiled. "No babies today, thank goodness. Mom would freak out if they came before she got home."

"That's exactly what Kellie and I were just discussing." He leaned over the side of the bed that wasn't occupied with nurses, drips, and wires to give his wife a kiss. "Hi beautiful. How's my girl?"

She lifted her free hand to caress his face. "I'm good, now that you're here."

"Are you in any pain?"

"Not a bit. It feels a little strange to have everyone making such a fuss over me. They tell me it's down to mild spotting. Oh, thank you," she called out to the nurses as they left. Her eyes softened affectionately as she acknowledged her sister's entrance into the room. "Hey, sis."

Kellie approached Cat's bed and threw her arms around her. "You had me worried."

Cat shrugged. "Sorry, that was not my intention." She glanced at the door. "Is Brad outside with the kids?"

"Oh, hell no. Traveling with those two isn't our idea of fun. I fed Michael and put him down for a nap, and Brad was creating new artwork with Diana when I left" She flanked Cat on the opposite side of her bed. "So, how are my Godchildren? Are they prepared to behave themselves enough to stay in there a little longer?" She leaned over Cat to speak into her significant belly. "Or is Auntie Kellie going to have to lay down the law for you two munchkins?"

Cat placed her hands on the sheet-covered mound. "I'm going to try my best, Kel. If it looks like they're giving me any trouble, I'll call you so you can scare them back in there."

Zach couldn't keep his laughter at bay. "If it were that simple, we wouldn't be here."

"I guess not." Cat turned back to her sister. "Please tell me you didn't call mom. I don't want her to worry."

Kellie shot a look of nervousness in Zach's direction. "No, but we were considering it. I think we should wait until they're about to board the plane in Seattle. I'll call her around 8:00 tomorrow morning. They should be at the airport by then. That way, they'll know to come straight here after landing in Lake Coburn."

Cat sent a somber glance at her sister. "I think that's best. It'll cut out a lot of worry time on her part."

Kellie fidgeted under Cat's intense stare. She opened her purse and began scrounging for something. "Where's the nearest cold drink machine?"

Zach stood, sensing the sisters needed some girl time. "I've got it, Kellie. What do you want?"

"I'll take a diet tea if they have it. If not, a cup of water will do. Thanks Zach."

Cathryn waited several seconds after her husband left the room before turning back to her sister. "I want to talk to you about something."

Her sister's face fell. "Oh hell, I knew there was something. My 'Spidey Senses' were tingling."

Cat scraped her teeth along her lower lip. She took a deep breath and released it slowly. "I have this feeling, Kellie."

Kellie's eyes widened with undisguised fright. "Are you cramping? Let me get the nurses."

Cathryn shook her head. "Not that kind of feeling. It's just . . . I don't know. I'm afraid, sis."

Kellie's hand flew up in front of her face. "I don't want to hear any of this from you." She pointed at Cat's belly. "You and those babies are going to be fine!"

Cat's tone sounded serious. "If anything happens to m   "

"Nothing is going to happen. You're being paranoid."

"Kellie!" She waited until her sister had settled into her fine-I'll-listen-if-you-insist stance—arms crossed stubbornly against her torso. "If anything happens to me, do *not* let my husband blame himself. This is no one's fault."

Kellie's eyes welled with tears. She sat, deflated, upon her sister's bed. "What's got you thinking this way? What exactly is it that you see happening?"

Cat shook her head. "Something—not good. I'm sorry. I can't explain it any better than that." She relaxed suddenly, settled back into her pillow. "But, it's okay now that I've told someone. *If* something happens, I'll know that you'll tell Zach what he needs to know, right? It's not his fault."

Kellie wiped her eyes and nodded. "Okay, but don't expect me to tell him to 'find someone else' to be happy with, because that'd more than I could bear."

Cat sent her sister a sad smile. "That won't be necessary."

"Oh . . . well, good then."

Kellie beamed, obviously mistaking her older sister's meaning. Cat decided to let it go. She got what she wanted. As for the other, she suspected that without her, Zach would spend the majority, if not the rest of his life without a partner. Just as she would do, if something ever happened to him. She closed her eyes and took a moment to pray that whatever happened, he'd have their children, and grandchildren, and great grandchildren, to fill his days with joy and laughter.

Was she overreacting? Was it just that infamous hormonal 'pregnancy paranoia' her mom had always insisted she'd suffered from?

God, she hoped so.

May 30th – 35 weeks and 1 day
T minus 35 days, and counting

Ellen and Gavin Barton rushed through the door of the OB unit, both barely recovered from their Alaskan cruise and flight home. In several long strides, Zach joined Cat's mom and step-dad. He hugged Ellen, whose face revealed lines of worry over her daughter's condition. "Hey, mom, Doc Barton. You two must be beat."

"And worried," Ellen added. "How is Cathryn? Are she and the twins in any danger?"

"Not at the moment. She's been spotting some but they're keeping a close eye on her. Dr. Brown and his teams are fully prepared to take the babies sometimes this week."

Doc Barton wrapped his arms around his wife's midriff from behind. "Is he certain about what's causing the bleeding?"

Zach nodded. "She has no sign of abdominal pains. Her ultrasound shows the cervix is more than halfway blocked and she's significantly effaced. He says it's slightly more common in pregnancies involving multiples. He wants her here where he can monitor her."

"So there's zero chance of a normal delivery at this point." Ellen looked from Zach to her husband, as though one of them could tell her differently.

"Sounds to me like that ship has sailed." Gavin looked apologetically at his wife.

"It has, sir. Dr. Brown insists that attempting to deliver a baby that way would only cause severe blood loss."

The other man gave his wife a comforting hug. "He's right, Ellen. A Caesarean section is much safer under these conditions, for both Cathryn and the babies."

Ellen seemed to process the information and come to a decision to accept it, for better or worse. She looped her arm around Zach's waist and plastered a smile on her face. "Caesarean delivered babies are always so much prettier, Zachary. Their little heads are perfectly shaped from not having to pass through the birth canal. She'll be fine, you'll see."

"I think so too, but you know your daughter as well as I do. She's still disappointed. Said she was looking forward to the experience of labor."

Ellen cringed. "That's not something you hear every day. I guarantee, if she only knew how difficult some of them are, she'd be thankful to skip it. You know, I carried Cat with no trouble, but hemorrhaged for Kellie. Kellie did for her first, and now Cat is threatening. It makes me wonder if there's a genetic weakness carried by the women in my family." She took a step toward the door. "Can we see her now?"

"They're changing her sheets, but they should be finished soon. Damn, if y'all had shown up ten minutes earlier you could have met the team Dr. Brown assembled. They left a few minutes before you came in."

The room cleared and Zach entered his wife's home away from home for the next two days. "Hey babe, look who's here to see you?" It did him good to see the light in her eyes as she caught sight of her visitors.

"Mom!"

Ellen rushed to her daughter's side, throwing her arms around her. "How are you, Sweet Pea?"

"I'm good." Overcome with emotion, Cat's face crumpled into a teary mess.

Zach snapped a handful of tissues and hurried to the bed to support his wife as she cried. "It's fine now, sweetie. Your mom's here."

Cat wiped her eyes with the tissues and blew her nose. "I'm just so relieved. I was so afraid I wouldn't get to see you before . . . before the babies were born," she muttered through tearful hiccupping. "I wanted you here so badly."

"Oh honey, not as much as I wanted to be here. I didn't think the stupid flight out of Seattle would ever end. If that wasn't enough to wrack my nerves, they delayed it over an hour and we nearly missed our connecting flight from Houston. I thought I was going to have a stroke. Gavin was calm through it all, but I was frantic."

Cat found the ability to smile at her step-dad through her tears. "Good ole, Pops. You had it all under control, didn't you?"

He leaned over and gave her a kiss on the cheek. "I sure did. If we'd missed that flight I would have hired a friend of mine to fly us back in a smaller plane." He adjusted the collar of his polo shirt. "This old fart's got connections." He patted her hand and gave her an indulgent smile. "So, what's going on here?"

"I feel fine, Pops. No pain at all. Dr. Brown says the bleeding is minimal." Cat grabbed her mom's hand. She bit her lower lip as her large, liquid brown eyes filled with tears. "Did Zach tell you about . . .?" Her voice faltered.

Ellen nodded. "The delivery method, yes, he told me. I know it's not what you wanted but it'll be safest for all of you." She settled next to her daughter on the bed.

Zach cleared his throat. "And your mom assures me that our babies will be exceptionally handsome because of it. No misshapen little cone heads for our sons." He recognized the flash of challenge in his wife's expression. *Mission accomplished.*

"Silly daddy, our *daughters* will be beautiful, regardless of how they are born."

Ellen voiced her own opinion on the matter. "Personally, I hope you have one of each, so we don't have to hear one of you gloat over who guessed correctly for the rest of our lives. Now tell me, did anything happen to bring this on? A fall, or a slip, or something?"

"No, ma'am. We were doing a little shopping at the Home Improvement store before her doctor's appointment—"

"I wanted to look for a rug for the nursery," Cat volunteered. "I had to go to my doctor's appointment, anyway, so I figured we'd leave the house a little early and take care of that first."

"So, this happened before the doctor's appointment?"

"Yes, ma'am. She's had a slight case of cabin fever, and was adamant about wanting to pick it out herself. I made sure she was in that wheelchair the entire time, except when she got up to go to the restroom. That's when she noticed the bleeding."

Ellen rolled her eyes. "Lordy, if you aren't every bit as stubborn as your father was."

Her husband's brow furrowed before he cocked his head at his wife. "No possibility she could get that from you, huh?"

Ellen turned to him. "I don't think I'm stubborn at all."

Pops smiled smugly. "Keep telling yourself that, sweetie."

Cat grinned at her step-dad's comment, thankful her mom had found someone to fill the emptiness from her dad's death over four years ago. "I am a little angry at myself for making Zach take me to Home Depot before my appointment. I really thought it would be okay as long as he was rolling me around in that wheelchair."

Zach leaned in to give his wife a tender kiss. "There's a good chance this would have happened even if we'd gone straight to the doctor's office." He wasn't about to make her feel worse than she already did. A soft knock on the door had Kellie entering.

"Hey, y'all got room for one more?" She entered and gave her mother and step-dad hugs. "I don't even have to ask about Alaska. I've been keeping up with all the pictures and video you've been posting on social media sites. It looked beautiful."

"It really was, but I'm ecstatic to be back. I missed my grandbabies. I bet they've grown three inches since I've been gone."

Kellie smiled at her mom and then turned a somewhat sober gaze upon her sister. "How are you, Cat?"

"I'm good, Kel."

Her brief answer had Zach wondering again at the silent signals being passed between the two siblings. The strange vibes had been strongest when he'd returned to the room after leaving them alone yesterday.

Kellie held up a yellow gift bag to her sister. "Here, I got you something. And can I say again how annoyed I am that you've refused to find out the sex of these babies?"

"I want to be surprised, Kel. Is that so bad? You know, our ancestors had babies all the time without finding out the gender."

Zach watched his wife's head fall back on her pillow, as though her speech had utterly drained her. Obviously, the visitation session was taking its toll on her body. A few more minutes and he'd suggest they let her get some rest.

Kellie continued her rant, giving her sister a pout. "But it's so much better if you know what colors to buy—pink dress for a little girl or a blue suit for a little boy."

"Buy a yellow or light green preemie onesie. Even those will swallow them for the first couple of weeks." Ellen brushed the hair back from Cat's forehead. "But they'll fatten up in no time. I have a feeling they'll be tall, like their daddy." She rested her head against her daughter's bed and addressed Zach. "As I recall, you were a pretty big boy as a toddler. Your mom always said if they'd had any more children, they'd have to take out a loan to keep you fed."

"I was a growing boy."

"You still were all the many afternoons you spent at our house when you and Cat were 'best friends'. I always cooked extra if I knew you were going to be coming by. Paul used to say *"If Zach shows up for a meal, there's a damn good chance someone else will leave the table hungry."*

Kellie spoke under her breath to her stepdad. "And let me tell you, Pops. That was pretty much every day, since he had a serious case of wood for my sister all those years."

Ellen gasped as Zach and Doc stifled their laughter. "Kellie Joanne, watch your mouth!"

"Oh come on, Mom. It was as true then as it is now. Everyone in town knew it except for Cat. All of that 'best friend' talk—what a load of crap."

Ellen shook her head in distaste. "Well, call it a crush or something, rather than, you know. Honestly, that is so crass."

Zach chuckled at his mother-in-law's discomfort. "I can't argue with any of that. Cat has always been the only girl for me. And I loved every minute I got to spend at your house, especially after my mom passed away." He patted his belly and laughed. "All those good meals you fed me helped to make me the man I am today."

A look of sadness passed over Ellen's face, as though remembering years gone by. "Elizabeth would have adored having grandchildren. And Paul, too." She accepted the hand her new husband offered and gave it a comforting pat, before smiling up at Zach. "I've thought about your mom so many times since you came back into Cat's life. I miss that sweet lady so much."

He nodded at the woman his mom had considered one of her dearest friends and remembered the hug she'd given him at the funeral, telling him if he ever needed to talk, she was there for him. He'd taken her up on it a couple of times, too. "I miss her too, Ms. Ellen. I've been thinking about her a lot, lately."

"I guess it's natural, at a time like this, to think of those we've lost." Ellen swiped a tear from the corner of one eye. "But, we should be remembering how ecstatic both Liz and Paul would be if they were here. Not one, but two new grandchildren coming in to the world. Speaking of which, where's your dad?"

"He and Paw Paw spent the night in Houston. Pop had to bring him to his cardiologist for a test yesterday and stayed for today's follow up appointment to get the results. I told him to get Paw Paw home and rested this evening. They'll be here tomorrow morning."

He glanced over at his wife. Her eyes were closed. "I guess we need to let this one get some rest. It's hard work carrying around two babies, even from a hospital bed." When he leaned in to give her a kiss, her head fell limply to the side. "Cat?" He picked up her hand, and it fell, unresponsively, to the sheet.

"Is she sleeping?"

A slow building panic rose steadily in his chest at Kellie's question. "Cathryn?" He touched her face—still no response. *Not sleeping.* Zach was reaching for the call button when the monitors seemed to go crazy with shrill beeps. "What the hell?"

"What's happening?" Ellen shrieked.

Panic gripped at his chest as something caught his eye. A pinkish stain seeping through the previously crisp, white linens.

Doc Barton pushed him aside to rip the top sheet back, revealing a horrifying pool of dark crimson. Everyone in the room drew in a single, collective gasp as he pushed the call button.

"Oh dear God . . ." Zach barely recognized his own voice as nurses swarmed the room, ordering everyone out and pushing him aside.

4:58 p.m. – Baby A

"Baby A is a girl, attached to her own placenta. This is the one that was blocking the cervix." Dr. Brown lifted the infant to her pediatric team and went in for the second one.

"There's so much blood . . ." Zach hadn't realized he'd spoken the words aloud until he heard the reply.

"She's got a bleeder but I'm going to fix that."

Still, Zach stared at the scene, wondering how anyone could lose that much blood and survive.

4:59 p.m. – Baby B

"And here's Baby B—it's a boy."

"Mother's BP is dropping!"

"Take him." Dr. Brown passed off the infant to the second team and turned his attention to its mother. "She's going into shock. Push those fluids. What's her pressure?"

Time froze for Zach, able to focus only on the hands of the team working over his wife. He watched the continual rush of removal and replacement involving her poor body. And through it all, his panic level continued to rise to dangerous levels, threatening to suffocate him. *I can't lose her.*

"Zachary!"

The command jarred him. He lifted his gaze from Dr. Brown's blood covered surgical gloves to the mask covering his face.

"Talk to her, Zachary. Make her hear you."

"BP is 42 over 26! We're losing her!"

Day 1: D-Day

Zach exited the double doors wearing his scrubs and what he was sure was an expression of equal parts awe and terror. Nothing—absolutely nothing—could have prepared him for what he'd experienced in that last twenty minutes of chaos.

Ellen was the first to see, as well as approach him. "How is she? Are the babies all right? Is my daughter all right?"

"One girl. One boy. Five pounds, twelve ounces and five pounds, eight ounces—respectively. They're fine. Lungs seem to be fully developed. Cathryn . . ." His voice faltered. "She's lost a lot of blood. They're asking for donations if any of you are matches."

"But is she okay, Zach?"

He didn't know how to answer that. "I-I think so, mom."

"I'm a universal type and it's been long enough since my last donation." Doc Barton headed toward the nurse's station.

Kellie stepped forward. "I'm B positive, the same blood type as Cat. Hey Pops, will they let me donate this soon after having a baby?" She headed off after her step-dad.

That left Zach staring down at his mother-in-law, her tear-filled eyes wide with worry.

"Tell me."

"It was bad, mom. Really bad." He wiped at his face with one hand. "There was so much blood. But they took the girl first, then the boy. Those two teams whisked them off so fast I barely got to see them. And then . . . then they started working on Cat, pumping blood into her, fluids into her, trying to get her blood pressure back up. It was so low . . . I don't know how anyone can survive having their blood pressure drop that low."

Ellen grabbed his arm, hanging on for dear life.

He swallowed the sob that threatened at the awful memory stabbing at him. "I think—I mean—I *know* she—left us—for a while. They gave her a shot of adrenaline and did chest compressions. Dr. Brown told me to talk to her. So I did. I held her hand and kept yelling at her not to leave me." He covered his mouth, shaking his head as he attempted to recover some semblance of control. "And she did, mom. She finally came back to me."

Ellen released a low sob and nodded vigorously. "Of course she did. She would do anything you asked her to do, Zachary. That's how much she loves you."

"Oh God. I came so close . . . so damn close to losing her. All I could think of was how much I love her. How I didn't think I could live without her. So that's what I told her."

Ellen seemed to gain strength from his words, even as he revisited the terror. Shoulders back and head up, she squeezed his arm. "But you didn't, and that's what matters. She'll be fine, my boy. She will, you'll see."

He nodded. "I know she will. No way would she leave this earth without seeing her babies. Our babies." His gaze locked with the grandmother of his children. "I'm a father."

Her laughter shot forth in a hysterical burst. "Yes. Yes, you are. A double whammy. And I have two more grandchildren. Four now, of who knows how many."

Her words had a sobering effect on him. "If I have any say in the matter, that's it for us. I don't ever want to see her in this kind of danger again."

"I can certainly see your point. But every pregnancy is different. The next time around could be perfectly normal. But, I suppose it could be why God gave you two at a time." She reached out and gave Zach a comforting hug. "Everything for a reason, son-in-law." She released him quickly, pointing behind him. "Here's the doctor."

Dr. Brown approached, stripped of the blood covered scrubs Zach had last seen him in. He thanked the man silently, knowing it would have driven Cat's mom and sister over the proverbial edge. God knows the sight of Cat's blood over every surface had nearly done him in.

The doctor pulled off his scrub cap and ran a hand through his hair. "She gave us a scare, but your wife's situation is stabilized now. Her vitals are very good. Her blood pressure is still extremely low, but that'll improve as the blood transfusions progress. We're pushing that IV as fast as it'll go for fluids."

Doc Barton approached and addressed his colleague. "How many units of blood have you ordered?"

"Up to five, and we'll reassess to see if she needs more. She's wrapped in thermo sheeting and we're keeping a close eye on her." He turned to Zach and placed a hand on his shoulder. "I know it was rough in there for you, but you did your job, Zachary. You kept her *here*—right where she belongs."

"You think she'll fully recover from the blood loss, right?" Zach's heart couldn't take anything more than a solid yes.

"Absolutely. She's a strong young woman. She'll be all perked up and good as new in about six hours." He grinned at the new daddy. "You're the father of twins now, Mr. Ferguson. You've got bigger troubles ahead of you."

Zach nodded, as sweet relief washed over him, lightening his burden. "How are they?"

"The pediatricians will be out here to discuss their conditions with you shortly. As you can imagine, they've got their hands full at the moment." He smiled at the new father. "But, you've got two beautiful, healthy babies. You heard them squawking right? Protesting when I took them out of that cozy environment in there? If those lungs aren't already fully developed, I'll eat my scrub cap."

Day 2 (6:00 AM): Baby A and Baby B

(13 hours old)

Zach sat in the semi-dark hospital room, staring down at his beautiful daughter. From his perspective, she had all the signs of being a looker like her mama. "I still can't believe we're parents."

"I know, right? It's like, if you look up the meaning of surreal in Webster's Dictionary, this would be it." Cat adjusted her son's head in an attempt to start him nursing again.

"You need more pillows?"

"No. I just need him to latch on. Come on sweetie, you can do this." Another adjustment had her smiling. "There it is. That's a good boy."

"Ah, he's a breast man, just like his daddy."

Cat rolled her eyes as her husband chuckled. "We can't call them Baby A and Baby B forever, you know. We need to give these munchkins their own names."

Zach smiled as his infant daughter curled her tiny fingers around his pinky. "I've been thinking about that. We could use names that start with the same letter."

"Like Thing 1 and Thing 2?"

"Or Frick and Frack," he offered.

"Tit and Tat," she snorted.

He laughed softly, so as not to jar the baby he held. "How about . . . Mabelle and Moses?"

Cat sent him a look that would fry eggs. "Be serious, would you? Let's find something that won't make them want to kill us in our sleep once they hit puberty."

Zach sent his wife an indulgent smile. "Okay, let's start with the letter A. Alfred and Alice."

"Alfred? Like Batman's butler? I don't think so. Abigail and Alex."

"Abigail sounds like a cat name to me. Bruno and Betty."

"Mars and Rubble? I think not. Caleb and Cassandra."

"Hm, that has a nice ring to it. But let's not lock ourselves in just yet. Daniel and Debbie, no, not Debbie, because if she ever moved to Dallas . . . n-n-no. Denise. Daniel and Denise."

She wrinkled her nose adorably. "I'd always think of Daniel Tiger from that kid show. Ethan and Elise."

He squinted in concentration. "Spell the girl name."

"E-L-I-S-E."

He shook his head. "Everyone would call her Elsie, like the cow, and you damn well know it."

"Erin, then?"

"*Erin go Bragh?* Hell no! Our Scottish ancestors would disown us."

"Francis and F-f-f-f-f . . . nope, I got nothing," she admitted.

"Garret and . . .Gloria?"

She shook her head this time. "I like the C's. Caleb and Cassandra."

"Is your heart set on it?"

Cathryn nodded. "It kind of is, and we could give them our parents' names too. Caleb Paul and Cassandra Elizabeth."

Zach frowned. "The boy name is fine, but that girl name—can you imagine the pressure she'd feel having to learn to spell that? We could shorten it to Beth."

"But your mom's name was Elizabeth."

He shrugged. "My pop never called her anything but Beth or Bethie for as long as I can remember. I can live with Cassandra Beth." Zach loved watching his wife's eyes soften visibly when he said or did something that touched her soul. "I know that look. Did I do it for you, babe?" He stared at her luscious lips, captivated by the subtle lifting of the corners.

"You certainly did." She looked at her son. "What do you think, huh Baby B? Would you prefer to be Caleb Paul Ferguson, after my dad? He was your Paw Paw Paul." The infant stopped nursing, turned his head slightly toward the sound of her voice, before latching on again. She turned her tearful gaze upon her husband. "He likes it."

"Of course he does. Caleb Paul Ferguson and Cassandra Beth Ferguson—two fine names. What's not to like?"

"I love you, Zach-attack."

"I adore you, Cat-astrophe."

Day 2: Cassandra and Caleb: 15 hours old
Full Circle

Cathryn heard a soft knocking at the door and looked up. "Come in." She beamed at the sight of an older version of Zach peeking inside. She'd always adored Zach's dad. The man stood, holding his best summer cowboy hat, and wearing the trademark Ferguson grin. "Hey there, Mr. Johnny. Or should I say Paw Paw Johnny? Wash your hands first and then come on over here and introduce yourself to one of your grandchildren." She watched, as he did as told. Her son was already a handsome little man. But she prayed he'd grow into the same good looks as his father and grandfather, right down to the coal black hair and piercing blue eyes.

Finished with his task, he approached the bed and gave her a gentle hug. "How's my favorite daughter-in-law doing?"

"Docs it still count if I'm your only daughter-in-law?" She kissed him on the cheek.

"It absolutely counts. I could have twenty of 'em and you'd always be my favorite. Which one do we have here? Scratch that, he's swaddled in blue so this must be my new grandson." He took the infant carefully and sat in the chair nearest her bed. "Hey, young man. I'm your grandfather. But you can call me Paw Paw John."

"Excuse me, but that tagline's been taken already, boy."

Cathryn smiled at the even older version of her husband standing in the doorway. Other than lacking the full head of hair, as well as physical height that both his son and grandson possessed, the family resemblance was astounding. "Hey Paw Paw John."

"Exactly!" He nodded and pointed a thumb at his own chest. "*I'm* the only Paw Paw John in this family." He puffed out his chest to his son. "You gotta be oldest and ugliest to get dibs."

Cat waved off his comment. "Pfft, there you go fishing for compliments again, Paw Paw. You know darn well there's not an ounce of ugly on you."

"Ugly is as ugly does," the younger John added. "And pop, it's not my fault that five consecutive generations of Fergusons displayed a complete lack of imagination in naming their sons. That's why Beth and I steered clear of it when we had one. Zachary is a nice, strong, perfectly acceptable name. And more importantly?" He leaned forward to make his point. "It's not John."

The older John chuckled as he greeted Cathryn at the bed and kissed her forehead fondly. "Forget him. How's my girl? Had a rough time of it, I hear."

She gave him a one shouldered shrug. "I'm good, still a little weak, and they limit my nursing sessions, but I'm getting stronger all the time."

The older John's arthritic hand lingered on her head for a moment. He stared at her with eyes the same shade of blue as her husband's, although slightly cloudy from age.

He blinked several times and finally gave her a satisfied nod. "Good to know." He inspected the room. "Where's the other one? I didn't come here prepared to wait my turn. Hell, I thought I'd have my own bundle of joy to hold."

Cathryn chuckled, appreciating the quick-wit and sharp sense of humor of her children's great-grandfather more than ever. "She's in the nursery. Her pediatrician is doing some blood work and running tests to make sure everything is as good on the inside as it is on the outside. She should be back soon."

Zach pushed open the door, carrying a large cup of coffee in one hand and a bottle of orange juice in the other. "Hey, we got us a party going on in here, or what?"

"Now we do. Hey grandson, that's a handsome little man you've got there."

"Yes sir, I have to agree with you." He shook his grandfather's hand and pulled him close for a one-armed hug. "Just wait until you see our daughter, Paw Paw. She's going to be every bit as pretty as her mama."

"A looker already, huh?"

"You bet." Zach moved to his father who sat admiring his new grandson. He bent at the waist, resting his hands on his thighs to watch his sleeping son. "What do you think, Pop?"

"Well, Zachary—" John Michael Ferguson blinked several times to clear his eyes as he and his son shared in a mutual show of emotion. "I think I can get used to this. Real quick. Congratulations, son."

Zach beamed at his father and accepted the hand shake he offered. "Thanks."

All eyes pivoted toward the doorway as the pediatric nurse entered, pushing the portable bassinet into the room. "Here's the other half of the dazzling duo. We'll leave them in here to visit for another thirty minutes or so."

Cat waved at the woman. "Thank you, Ms. Jackie."

John, the younger, stood to get a better look at his granddaughter. He grunted then cast a glance his son's direction. "Oh man. Are you ever gonna be in trouble in about fourteen years, son."

Zach snorted. "I hear that." He reached out for his son and turned to his grandfather who was finishing up with his hand-washing, obviously anticipating his turn. "Paw Paw, you want to hold your great-grandson?"

John David Ferguson, the elder, deposited the paper towel into the trash receptacle and turned, wearing a gleeful expression. "Well, hell yeah. Why else would I have suffered through your dad's bad driving skills?" He took over the chair the younger John had previously occupied and clapped his hands together. "Hand him over."

Cathryn's heart nearly burst with pride as Zachary's grandfather held her son for the first time. Remarkably, the infant's eyes opened wide and stared into the older man's face, as though studying him, or committing to memory, every laugh line, every wrinkle, and every work worn surface. Tears pooled and made their own trails down her cheeks. The current scenario did so much to warm her heart, filling the gap left by her own missing father. *If I can't have dad here, at least I have this.*

Paw Paw John chuckled as he checked out her baby boy. "Hello, young man. What's your name?"

"Caleb . . ." Cathryn spoke, barely over a whisper. "Caleb Paul Ferguson."

Without looking up, John David nodded and smiled. "Paul, after your father. I'm glad." He adjusted his hold on the child. "Caleb Paul Ferguson," he repeated. "That's a fine name for my great-grandson."

Cat turned as Zach's dad, John Michael, cleared his throat loudly. She watched him gently lift her daughter from the bed and cradle her in his arms. His gaze ricocheted from his granddaughter, to his daughter-in-law several times. Finally he smiled, nodding in obvious approval.

"Yep, she's got her beautiful mother's features written all over her." He walked over to the chair next to where his father sat, holding Caleb, and seated himself. "What's her name?"

Cat held her breath as Zach answered his father's question.

"Her name is Cassandra, Pop—Cassandra Beth Ferguson."

John Michael's eyes widened, obviously pleased, as he met Cathryn's tearful gaze. "Beth . . ." His voice broke as he cleared it and continued. "Bethie would love that. Thank you, Cat."

Cathryn nodded, unable to stem the steady flow of tears. She gratefully accepted the tissue her husband handed her, was more grateful for his presence as he grasped her hand and sat beside her on the bed.

Cathryn's emotions bubbled over in a plethora of feelings—proud, privileged, and truly blessed for being able to witness these most special of moments. She regretted being too out of it last night to see her own mother's initial reactions to her newest grandchildren. She suspected her mom had shed more than a few tears, and that Kellie had not been able to stop smiling.

But this—this presence of four generations of Fergusons, sharing this space, at this same moment in time—this was something special. It was almost as if they'd come full circle; the old, melded with three younger generations, to form an entirely new sense of reality for all of them.

And she was lucky enough to be a part of it.

A Memory for John Michael

John Michael checked the time, realized their visit was nearly over. "Before we go, I'd like to hold them both at the same time. May I?" He grunted in satisfaction as Zach placed Caleb in the crook of his free arm. His gaze flipped continuously from one to the other, noticing the various differences and similarities of facial features between his two grandchildren. "Look at 'em, just look at 'em, would you?"

John David, the elder, walked over to his son, and chuckled. "Yep, that's an armload of pooters, right there."

John Michael nodded and laughed in agreement. He heard a soft knock at the door, but didn't bother to look up. Another in the continual flow of nurses or techs, he supposed, who'd attended his daughter-in-law's every need. He blocked out all conversation as he concentrated all his attention on his two beautiful grandchildren.

"Don't you look good holding those two?"

The pleasant female voice broke into his silent reverence of the two infants. "Probably not as good as I feel, but thanks anyway." He looked up, grinning, and did a double-take at the woman standing before him. "Cynthia?" He squinted, to make sure he was seeing correctly.

With hands resting on her trim hips, the woman smiled and nodded. "I would have known you anywhere, John Michael. I swear, other than that silver sprinkled in your hair, you look exactly the same." She crossed her arms. "You suck for that, you know."

"Cynthia Anne Robicheaux?"

The pretty redhead's green eyes sparkled with laughter. "Nobody's called me that in a long time." She touched the name tag clipped to her lab coat's lapel. "It's Ellender now. I married a man from Oklahoma."

He frowned, trying to recall having seen her in the past 40 years since graduating high school. "Is that where you've been all this time?"

She nodded. "Two weeks after graduation, I took a bus to Oklahoma to spend a month with my grandparents. I met Gene my fourth week there and never returned."

"Until . . .?"

"Six months ago. I lost Gene last year and our three kids have scattered to different parts of the continent. I figured I'd come back on this end and spend some time with mom while I still can."

"I'm sorry about your husband." He smiled as he remembered a particular incident. "Your mom used to bake the best red velvet cake I've ever had. Oh man, that pudding-like filling, and cream cheese icing. Damn, it was good."

Cynthia nodded exuberantly. "She still does."

The elder John cleared his throat and spoke up. "Robicheaux? Are you Ham and Bess's daughter?"

"Yes sir, do you remember me?"

He slapped his thigh and laughed. "I sure do. I remember you tagging along with your dad everywhere he went."

"I bugged you mercilessly to see those new chicks every time you got in a new batch." She went over to give him a hug. "How are you Mr. John?"

He nodded. "I'm good. And Johnny's right about your mother's red velvet cakes. That's when people baked 'em from scratch. Not these crappy mixes that don't have any taste." He shook his head. "It broke my heart not to make your dad's funeral a few years back. I was with my wife at Lourdes Hospital in Lafayette. She was fighting her own battle with the big 'C' at the time."

Cynthia's face dropped. "Oh. Did she . . .?"

"No, she beat the cancer. But sometimes I wonder if . . ." He stopped, wiped his mouth with his hand.

John Michael met Cynthia's curious gaze. "Mom has late stage Alzheimer's," he explained.

"I'm so sorry." She reached out to his father, touched his arm gently. "Have you looked into the groups here for the families of those afflicted with the disease? Sometimes it helps to talk about it with others in the same situation."

He cleared his throat with a loud harrumph. "Thanks, maybe I'll look into that."

John Michael and Zach exchanged looks equal in their levels of skepticism. Both implying, *Yeah, old man, sure you will.*

"So . . ." Cynthia swiveled and pointed to Zachary. "You're the father, obviously. You look too much like John Michael not to be his son."

"I am, and extremely proud of it."

"Well, I need to speak to both you and your wife about a particular procedure for," she checked at her paperwork, "Caleb."

"What procedure? Is something wrong?" Zach's voice registered panic.

John Michael groaned. "I think she's asking about a circumcision, son."

Cynthia gave him a quick nod. "You are correct. I'm here to answer any questions the two of you may have on the procedure, or to help you decide, one way or another."

John David stood quickly, adjusting his belt buckle. "Holy crap. I know I don't need to be here for this conversation. Are you about ready to go, son?"

"Sure am, Pop. That's not anything I want to think about." John stood carefully, handed his granddaughter to Zach, and placed his grandson carefully back in his designated bassinet. "Poor little booger," he murmured, gently tucking his grandson's blanket around the tiny figure. "I hope they do a good job, for your sake. They can botch those things, you know." He looked up at a host of eyes upon him. "Well, not me. I'm just sayin'."

His dad snorted. "Well, looks to me like your sayin' ain't helpin' much. Let's go, boy. It might be best to make our exit before they start tossing stuff at us."

John grabbed his hat and nodded at everyone. "I'll be back tomorrow, probably without the old guy, since he finds my driving so appalling and all." He found Cynthia's eyes pinned to him. "Cyn," he said, slipping in the nickname he'd called her in high school. "It was good to see you."

"You too, John." She smiled again. "Maybe I'll see you again before they leave the hospital."

"I hope so." He ducked out of the room, grateful his old man had exited the room without witnessing the wink she'd sent him. That old fart would jump to foregone conclusions in a heartbeat. He pulled the door quietly closed, and turned, only to have his father in his face, wearing a smug expression.

"I gotta hit the head again, Johnny."

"Of course you do." He shook his head as his dad disappeared into the men's restroom. He stood there in the corridor, twirling his truck keys in his hands for a minute or two, thinking about that wink Cynthia had given him. What exactly, if anything, had she meant by that?

"You're still here."

He spun on his heel to see her approach, wearing the same smile that had captivated him all through high school. "Waiting on Pop, as usual." He used his thumb to point at the restroom door. "His second home, lately."

"Enlarged prostate, huh?"

"Yeah, but don't let him hear you say that. He's in denial." He smoothed the rim of his hat trying to come up with a better topic of conversation.

"Those are two beautiful grandchildren you have in there. Are they your first?"

He nodded. "If Zach has anything to say about, they'll be my last. He almost lost that sweet girl in there."

"I know. I heard it got serious in the delivery. It's remarkable how well they've adjusted to the environment outside the womb, though. Not a single sign of respiratory distress, none of the usual complications to babies of premature birth. Mother and babies are perfectly fine. There's no reason to believe her next pregnancy will be troublesome. Each one is different."

He waved his finger between the two of them. "We know that, but who's going to convince my son?" He shrugged. "Of course, if Cat wants more children, I have a feeling they'll have another go round at it. So, what did they decide about the procedure?"

She grinned. "Helmet head."

John winced. "Poor little guy. When?"

"Since they were a month early, I've advised them to wait a couple of weeks. They'll decide whether to bring him back here, or use their own pediatrician, or even use a specialist."

He cocked his head at her answer. "I didn't realize the medical profession had circumcision specialists." Her laughter rang out between them.

"Well, not specifically for that, but a pediatric urologist. Whomever they choose, your grandson will be fine." She grabbed her buzzing phone and read the text. "I need to be somewhere." She slipped it back into her pocket and grinned at him. "You know, some of my best memories from home involve your dad's feed store."

He nodded. "The shipments of chicks, I know."

She lifted one shoulder. "Yes . . . and those hay bales." Lifting her hand, she wiggled her fingers in a wave. "See you around, John Michael."

She spun on her heel and walked at a brisk pace away from him. She'd always been a tiny little thing, and from the looks of it, she still was.

He turned, paced an impatient trail in front of the restroom door, waiting for his father.

He froze in his tracks. *Hay bales.* Suddenly, a memory flooded his mind, as vividly as if it had happened yesterday, instead of forty years ago.

He'd spent all afternoon unloading a trailer full of hay bales. She'd shown up with her dad toward the end of it and offered to help. When he said he didn't need help from a girl, she'd hung around to watch. He'd nearly busted a gut trying to impress her with his speed and strength at handling the bales. He couldn't exactly remember the details, but somehow he'd ended up kissing Cyn behind the widest, tallest stack he could find. He'd forgotten all about the late summer event that had provided him with enough fantasizing to last all throughout junior high and most of high school.

John swiveled in the direction she'd headed, just in time to see her turn back for a second look at him. Still within earshot, he caught her light-hearted laughter as she sent him a final wave and turned a corridor to disappear from view.

How the hell had he forgotten Cynthia Anne Robicheaux?

July 26th – 8 Weeks A.D. (After Delivery)
The Death of Medically Advised Abstinence

"Hello beautiful. What's up?"

Cat smiled at her husband's phone salutation, knowing she was about to deliver a message that would rock his world. "You need to get home, Zachary. You need to get home—now."

"Oh . . . God. Really?"

"Yep."

"I was about to head home anyway. I'll be there in five minutes."

"Don't kill yourself getting over here. I'm too horny to handle widowhood with any kind of class. But hurry."

"Babe, I'm already in the truck."

As proof, she heard the roar of his engine. "See you in a bit." Cathryn ended the call. She dabbed Zach's favorite perfume on her pulse points, checked her appearance in the mirror one more time before exiting the master bath.

Nearly three months.

That's how long it had been. Three *long* months since she'd made love to her husband, due to unforeseen complications. Ah, but tonight the medically advised abstinence would come to an abrupt halt. It couldn't happen too soon for her.

Everything was perfect. The house sparkled, she'd changed the sheets on the bed, even sprinkled the fitted sheet with a sinfully expensive perfumed powder that made them feel like silk. She'd lit candles an hour ago when she'd stepped into the shower. The master suite smelled luscious. Not that she even expected poor Zach to notice.

All day long she'd prepared for this. She'd hit up her mom and Poppa Doc to babysit so she could have one evening alone with her husband. She'd kissed her babies, sent them off with tons of supplies, including several bottles of milk she'd expressed, and many thanks to her mom and step-dad.

"Call me if anything goes wrong," she'd told them as they left with her two babies. She'd watched them drive off and took the time to utter a sincere plea that they wouldn't have to.

Folding back the sheets, she smoothed them out evenly, first one side, then the other. She gave the pillows a liberal plumping and went to watch for Zach. She heard the revved up engine of his truck before she actually saw him. He pulled into their driveway on two wheels and came to a skidding halt on the circular asphalt drive. Within seconds he'd pushed open the door and stood before her.

Reeking.

Smelling as though he'd taken a nose dive into a large pile of animal manure.

She put her hand to her nose. "Oh my God."

"I'm sorry. I made a delivery to the LeMaire's ranch. Their dog got in my way and I tripped. Fell in a pile of horse sh—"

"Stop. Shower. Now." She pointed behind him. "And for God's sake, take your boots off outside."

"Yes, ma'am."

She waved her hand in front of her face, suspecting all efforts to transform the master suite into a tropical paradise for their "first time" would be for nothing. Then she heard splashing from the shower in the mudroom.

Oh the sweet, considerate man.

Rather than bring the stench inside the rest of the house, he was using the shower relegated to hosing down their huge golden retriever, Zeus.

In less than five minutes, he appeared, with a towel wrapped loosely around his hips. He held up his finger. "That was just to get the stench off. Now I'm going to have a real shower." He whisked by so quickly he practically blurred. "Oh yeah," he said. "It's about to get real up in here."

She followed him down the hall into their suite, heard his low whistle as he caught sight of the effort she'd put into the scenario.

"Oh, *hell* yeah."

The comment came a second before he closed himself up in their bathroom, and three seconds before she heard the shower taps.

After another fifteen minutes, Cathryn was ready to take a sledge hammer to the door. She'd suffered through his longer than usual shower, and a couple of minutes of a blow dryer running.

"Zachary, what is taking you so long?"

The door opened immediately and he emerged in a cloud of pure, male sexiness. All traces of horse manure replaced by Tom Ford's *Extreme*. His torso fully exposed—traps, abs, and pectorals all tanned and perfectly toned from years of hard work, oftentimes shirtless. His coal black hair squeaky clean and glistening, his face completely free of a five o'clock shadow. God bless him. He knew she found a clean shave irresistible to the touch. Her gaze lowered to the navy blue towel tied loosely around his lean hips, but exposing the pads of muscle on either side. The towel dipped dangerously low in the front. She sucked in her breath as the front of the towel lifted of its own volition, visibly tenting his prominent arousal. "Oh. My. God."

Yeah . . . that's the look he wanted to see on his wife's face. Cat's eyes widened, obviously appreciating his efforts. Her lips parted, pink and panting, her skin flushed, and eyes bright with need. He could see her pulse, its rapid beating visible at the sexy hollow of her throat.

His beautiful Cat, standing there and wanting him, wrapped in the skimpiest robe she owned. She reached up to release the sash. His heart pounded, nearly exploded in his chest as the robe slipped off her arms, to fall in a puddle of aqua colored silk at her pedicured feet.

And there she was—completely bare and more beautiful than ever—all long legs, slender arms, and svelte body, with the tiniest bump on what used to be a perfectly flat belly. In his opinion, it made her sexier than ever. One hand made a slow trail to her hair, released the clip, allowing luxurious brown locks to cascade over smooth as satin shoulders.

"My God, you are beautiful."

The slight lift of her brow, the twitch of her mouth, the hitch in her breath—all clues he'd grown accustomed to—a veritable road map of her wants and needs. He knew what she wanted. His right hand moved to the corner of his towel and pulled, giving her an unobstructed view.

Her already pink cheeks flushed an even deeper pink as her mouth rounded in a taste tempting "O". "So are you."

They came together in an instant—fell to the bed, writhing in need, both anxious to fulfill the aching in their bodies, all thoughts of romance and taking it slow wiped out with their intense needs. Just as he was ready to slam into her, he came to a screeching halt, suddenly remembering all she'd been through. "Is this safe? I don't want to hurt you."

She groaned, pushed him onto his back and straddled him. "I sure as hell don't have a problem with hurting you."

Ten minutes later, they lay there panting and struggling to catch their breath.

Zach kissed his wife's neck. "Did I do it for you, babe?"

"Mm, hmm, that was every bit as good as our first time." She snuggled into his embrace.

"Next time I'll last longer," he panted.

She rested her hand on his chest and purred. "Good to know, because next time *I'll* last longer, too."

"Who's got the kids?"

"Mom and Pops."

"For how long?"

"Until tomorrow morning."

"Remind me to do something special for them."

"Like what? Flowers or taking them to dinner?"

"I was thinking more along the lines of season tickets to the Saints games."

She laughed. "That good, huh?"

"Absolutely." He turned, looped his arm around her to pull her close. Using the back of his hand, he ran a trail down the length of her side, stopping at the barely visible Caesarean scar. "I love this scar."

She released a hopeless sigh. "It's not going anywhere."

"It gave us our children."

She began a slow trail along his bare hip with one fingernail, and stopped at his groin. "I think you played a part in that, too."

"I may have had a supporting role, but you were the superstar." He reached for her hand, brought it to his mouth and kissed it tenderly. His heart expanded, choking him up, as it always did when he thought of those intense minutes in the delivery room. He swallowed the lump in his throat. By some tacit mutual agreement, neither of them had ever spoken of those traumatic moments. "We've never talked about what happened, Cat."

"I know."

"Do you want to know?"

"No, I mean, I know. I already know what happened."

"Did Dr. Brown tell you?"

She shook her head slowly. "No. I saw. I was aware that I was dying. I don't know how, but I was."

He frowned, more fascinated than curious about her admission. "What did you see?"

"I only saw and heard what went on in that room from my own body's point of view. I wasn't floating above or anything, the way some people describe it. But I knew I was leaving. I just didn't know where I was going. I wasn't worried, though. It was all so easy, so inviting." She slipped her arm around his waist and hugged him.

"And then I heard you, calling my name, telling me, begging me to come back to you, to fight for you and our babies. I heard lots of voices in that room— doctors, nurses, technicians—all of them loud and demanding. But when you spoke, it sounded almost like music that I could *see* as well as hear. Your voice was so soothing to my soul, and I knew neither of us would ever feel complete without the other. I knew somehow, I couldn't leave you."

Zach smiled, remembering something Ellen had said after that awful episode, when he was still shell shocked from nearly losing his wife. "That's how much she loves you." He met his wife's curious gaze. "That's what your mom said when I told her what happened. That you . . . left us."

He still couldn't get himself to say the word.

"But I called you back and you listened, you came back to me. Your mom said, 'Of course she did. Cat would do anything you asked her to do, Zachary. That's how much she loves you.' And I could only agree with her, because I knew it was true."

Cat propped herself up on one elbow and gazed down at him, her long lashes framing those liquid brown eyes, glistening with tears. "As long as I have any choice in the matter, I will always come back to you. *That's* how much I love you."

He rolled over, pinning her beneath him and kissed her, long and leisurely. "I adore you. And now that I've caught my second wind, I'm about to show you how much."

ABOUT THE AUTHOR

Photograph by Joan Granger of
Simple Memories Photography

Lori Leger lives in south Louisiana with her husband of nineteen years. Between the two of them, they have five wonderful children and a passel of grandchildren, ranging in age from two years to nineteen years of age. In March of 2012, she resigned an 18+year career in road design to write full-time. Lori is the owner and editor of Cajunflair Publishing Company. She has eight full-length novels, one novella, and five short stories published, with an article in a non-fiction book soon to be published. You can find Lori's works on *Amazon, Barnes and Noble, and Create Space.*

FIND ME:

Lori Leger's Website: http://www.lorilegerauthor.com
Facebook: http://www.facebook.com/llegerauthor
FB Page: http://www.facebook.com/lorilegerauthor
Twitter: http://twitter.com/lleger641
Blog: http://cajunflair.wordpress.com
Pinterest: http://pinterest.com/lleger641
Goodreads:
http://www.goodreads.com/author/show/5171074.Lori
 Leger

DEDICATION

To my husband, who continues to keep our home from falling down around us during my trips into deadline hell. I thank God for you every day. Your willingness to feed my caffeine habit with fresh cups of coffee prepared exactly to my liking, have propelled you to the hero hall of fame in my eyes. I love you, babe.

Also to the mothers of multiples out there, who are faced with the daunting challenge of raising more than one infant at a time. As one who has brought home two babies from the hospital to join their three year old sibling, God bless you. While I can't say it was easy, it was always interesting. I wouldn't change a second of it.

STAR CROSSED SUMMER SOLSTICE

By

Kellie Kamryn

Prologue

"Come on!" Five year old Kayla Webber tugged on the outstretched hand of her best friend, Kaleb Warner. "I want to play!"

With a firm grip on Kayla's hand, Kaleb sat still in the grass, nearly as immovable as the boulder beside him. "I have things to tell you."

"I know. You always have things to talk about." Kayla yanked her hand free, and skipped circles around Kaleb, her long blond hair ruffled by the wind. Then she hopped up onto the rock, arms stretched out wide. "We can talk after. Let's play!"

"This is important," young Kaleb insisted, holding out his hand to her again. "Our guardians could call us back at any time. I have to tell you something."

"I just got here. I won't have to leave yet." Kayla jumped off the large stone, and tumbled through the grass.

"Kayla!" Kaleb shouted.

Kayla cartwheeled to a stop in front of Kaleb, and stood with hands on her hips. "You grumpy?"

Thrusting his hand further in her direction, he urged her to take it. Kayla sighed, and grabbed hold of his hand.

Kaleb squeezed her tiny fingers with all of his might, hoping as only a sandy-haired five year old boy can, that he could get his playmate to listen to him. "I don't want you to forget me."

Kayla cocked her head in curiosity. "I wouldn't forget you. You're my friend."

"You might," Kaleb muttered.

"No way." Kayla shook her head, thin curls flying about her face.

"Well, don't. We have a lot of work to do."

"Sillyhead," Kayla giggled, tugging on his hand again. "Get up!"

Reluctant, Kaleb let Kayla pull him to his feet. "What do you want to play?"

"I wanna run!" Kayla squealed in delight and broke into a run, dragging Kaleb along behind her.

After a moment, Kaleb laughed, and ran full force beside her through the long, green grass, continuing to grip her hand in his.

When they reached the creek edge which ran through the property Kaleb resided on, they stopped, huffing and puffing from their efforts. Kayla glanced at Kaleb and he nodded. In silence, they picked up skipping stones, and proceeded to skim them across the water.

Did Dawn ever tell you the kissing hand story? Kayla directed her thoughts into Kaleb's head.

Kaleb threw a rock into the middle of the creek, watching the ensuing splash, counting the ripples. Curious, he tilted his head and nodded at Kayla to continue.

Marabel said that when we have to leave people we can kiss their hand and then they carry our love with them.

Intrigued, Kaleb squinted at his friend. *Really?*

Kayla nodded. *Uh-huh.*

Does it work?

Of course. Marabel said so.

Kaleb sighed. *I don't want you to leave.*

Kayla shrugged. *I have to some times. So do you. We always come back.*

Kaleb hung his head. *I know. But I don't like it when you're gone.*

Me neither. Kayla threw a rock as hard as she could to see how far it would go. She nodded in satisfaction when it almost reached the other side of the creek. *Marabel keeps telling me I have things to learn. I don't know what she means.*

Something about work. Kaleb's voice grumbled inside her head.

That's all the grown-ups talk about—work, Love, Light. Kayla tilted her face up to the sun, eyes closed, absorbing the heat into her skin. *I just wanna fly!*

I know you do. Kaleb chuckled inside her head. *One day.*

Kayla opened her eyes, and threw herself at Kaleb, wrapping her tiny arms around him. He squeezed her tight.

Here. Kayla broke their embrace and took hold of Kaleb's left hand. Lifting his palm to her lips, she placed a smooshy little girl kiss in the center. *I love you.*

Kaleb did the same to her hand. *I love you, Kayla.*

She grinned. *I know.*

I'll always fight alongside you. Kaleb followed his unspoken statement with a solemn nod.

Ya wanna play swords now? Kayla shoved away from him, and snatched up a nearby stick.

Kaleb laughed, his gaze searching the ground until he spied a tree branch a couple of feet away. Leaping over a rock, he grabbed it up and broke off a couple of stray twigs, then brandished his makeshift weapon. *Ready?*

Kayla giggled. *Yes!*

Chapter One

Despite the humid summer evening, Kayla Webber shivered as a sudden gust of wind feathered over her bare arms, and sent her chestnut hair flying out behind her. The full moon peeked from behind a bank of clouds, casting the landscape in an eerie glow. The occasional hoot of a night owl, interspersed with the sing-song of crickets, broke the silence.

Kayla quickened her steps, her knee-high black leather boots clacking against the sidewalk as she strode through the cemetery. A nervous laugh bubbled up from her gut. *How cliché.* What better way to meet your destiny than by the light of the moon surrounded by dead bodies six feet under?

Forcing out a breath, she willed her body to calm, her heart rate to slow. *Show no fear, show no fear.* Fear—an internal struggle she'd warred with since she'd been a child. *No reason to hurry, nowhere to run.* In fact, running wasn't an option. A battle loomed, one she'd trained for all her life.

What a way to usher in the summer solstice! I'd much rather be at home, lighting the candles in the garden, getting ready to dance under the full moon.

A wistful sigh escaped. Since she'd been a child, Kayla had known she was different. Memories of great campaigns had infiltrated her waking consciousness on a regular basis. Visions of other people, times, and places ran amok with her modern day life. She'd never known her biological parents. They'd given her up as a baby, and she'd been raised in a very special foster home for gifted children.

Gifted indeed. Smiling, she thanked the Lord and Lady of Light again for watching over her, allowing her guardians, Marabel Lovelace and Henry Wiseman, to find and raise her, teaching her to battle for the Light. Conquering demons and other worldly beings had been everyday occurrences during her upbringing. Spells, energy manipulation, and creating potions were integral to her education. Weird dreams of people and events that felt as real to her as the earth she walked on every day were a part of her reality.

For a moment, a vision of green eyes popped into her mind, ones she'd seen in dreams all of her life. She knew him as Kaleb Warner—his presence hovering somewhere in the ethers. She couldn't recall ever meeting him in person, but her guardians assured her that one day she would.

That day had yet to come. Sometimes she thought they'd all experimented with one potion too many.

Shaking her head, the image of Kaleb's eyes disappeared. She couldn't afford any category of distraction tonight. Swallowing hard, she pushed back the panic threatening to rise within her. *You can do this. You've done it before.* Inhaling a deep breath to calm her system, she sought to center her energy. *Only one difference tonight—I don't have any back up.*

When she'd fought demons in the past, her guardians had been close by and on full alert in case she needed them. Tonight—her first solo mission. Even though she'd trained for this night since she'd been a child, she still feared her inability to rise to the role she'd been born to play in this plane of existence. Her guardians told her she would understand her purpose when the time came; a phrase which grated on her nerves. Often, she felt incomplete, like she waited for something to come into her life to shine infinite universal wisdom onto her. Instead, it seemed as if the universe grinned at her, shaking its cosmic figurative head at her mere mortal musings.

Mid-stride, she paused, the air humming around her much akin to a wet fingertip running over a crystal wine glass. Her short, red leather skirt with built-in shorts—because it's far too difficult *not* to show your underwear while fighting in a skirt—flapped against her thighs in the breeze.

Drawing in a deep breath, the black leather of her crop top constricted against her chest. Just because she had a job to do for the Light, didn't mean she couldn't dress ready to kick butt. She accepted the cosmos didn't care about her style of dress. In a childish gesture, she stuck out her tongue. *Take that Universe.*

Closing her eyes, she stood with feet should-width apart, arms by her side, palms out, and summoned her Light. An invisible bubble of energy shielded her, head-to-toe. *This is it.* Heart pounding, she stood her ground, and waited.

Within seconds or minutes perhaps, two short sounds, like a needle scratching an old record player, caught her attention. Her eyes popped open wide.

With matted hair as black as night, facial features twisted in an evil grin, eyes glowing red, a demon reached out a claw, poking the invisible force field with a jagged fingertip, causing a crackling sound to permeate the air.

"How long do you think this will hold?" he rasped before breaking out in maniacal laughter.

Kayla snorted in derision. Shadow, or the darkness that resided in all human beings, was full of clichés—night battles that fed into the fears of the human mind, ugly demons laughing like crazed maniacs.

"Long enough for me to kill you," she quipped, wondering why she'd be faced with the likes of him since she'd been told tonight would be *special.* She'd battled worse during training. *What's the deal here?*

He cocked his head to the side. "They send a little girl to fight me, and she hides behind magic."

"Kiss my—" *Wait a minute.* There had been two *pops* which meant two demons. *Where is he?* Her intuition sensed someone behind her. Whirling on the spot, she sent out an extra energy burst to strengthen her shield.

Her heart pounded in her chest. "You!" She blinked in disbelief, her power wavering, shield faltering. *It can't be!*

"Yes," he growled. "Damn it . . . Hold your shield!"

Surprised by his command, Kayla sent another burst of energy from her hands. Taking in his bald head, smooth visage, and average height, her glance flicked over his black, fitted T-shirt, black jeans, and combat boots. She gulped, heart beating in an erratic rhythm. She stared into his eyes; eyes she'd seen in her dreams since she was a child. *Kaleb.*

"Better," he muttered. "I thought you were prepared for this."

His grumpy attitude got her back up. "I am prepared for *him*," she retorted. "I wasn't prepared for you. What are you doing…?" The energy bubble faltered along with her voice.

"Can we talk about this later?" he snapped, gesturing toward the demon still in front of her. "You've got a job to do!"

"You can't save her!" the demon barked.

Kaleb peered around Kayla to address the demon. "It's not my job to save her."

The less than thrilled tone of his voice irritated Kayla. *My hero.* She stared at him again. *I don't believe it.* In her visions, she and Kaleb had trained together. They'd had many conversations about anything and everything. She remembered other lifetimes with him where they were warriors, or children, or lovers. What was he doing here? She sent a plea to the Lord and Lady he wasn't a demon and she had to kill him.

"I'm not a demon," he stated, his mouth set in a grim line.

"Then how—"

"Later." He waved a hand in front of her. "Aren't you supposed to be a little too busy right now to talk?"

In an attempt to ignore him, she turned away from him, and focused her attention on the demon. *He's right. No time to figure this out now.* She'd meditate on it later.

With a swift, practiced movement, Kayla plucked a blade from the waist band of her skirt and flicked the knife at him, hitting him square between the eyes.

The demon screamed, stumbling back, clutching at the weapon embedded in his forehead. With a roar, he ripped the blade out of his flesh, a sickening squelch accompanying the motion.

Kayla swallowed hard. Mortal weapons couldn't defeat a supernatural being of his nature. They were only meant to slow down the demon until she could use her power on him. *Stay calm. You can do this.* However, Kaleb's presence had her questioning her ability to handle the situation. *Is this a test?* She straightened her spine. Test or no test, she had a job to do.

Tossing the blade to the side, the monster swiped at her with elongated claws. A zing resounded in the still night air as he penetrated the shield in front of her.

"Stay strong!" Kaleb ordered.

Grimacing, Kayla arched back, reaching for a dagger hidden inside her right boot. Brandishing the weapon, she ducked under the paw swipe of the demon, then drove the blade into his abdomen.

A screech rent the air as she withdrew the blade, and sliced open his thigh. The demon dropped to one knee, clutching at his wounds.

"Are you done slicing and dicing?" Kaleb growled from behind her.

Who the hell does he think he is? "A little help would be nice," she muttered.

"This isn't my fight."

Flicking a quick glance his way, she saw Kaleb standing with his arms crossed over his muscular chest, green eyes glinting in the moonlight. "Then save the commentary," she snarled.

Her momentary lapse in concentration weakened her force enough for the demon to swipe a hand through her shield, tearing at the tie between her breasts. Her leather bustier gaped open, revealing a red lace bra.

"That was my favorite top," she spat out. *At least the bra held.*

"Seriously, you're gonna lament a loss to your wardrobe at a time like this?" Kaleb's voice held a note of disbelief.

Ignoring the man behind her, Kayla figured it was now or never. Dropping her shield completely, she made a show of stabbing out at the demon again. The beast dug claws into the dirt, and dragged himself toward her. He made another swipe for her, leaving three slashes on the calf of her leather boot.

A scowl marred her features. "No one touches the boots." With the same wounded footwear, she kicked the demon in the bleeding wound on his forehead.

His head snapped back, and she used her other foot to shove at his chest. The demon fell to his back, but grabbed her ankle, pulling her down on top of him. *Right where I need to be.* She feigned fear, eyes wide, allowing her heart rate to increase. Mr. Big-Bad-and-Ugly flipped her to her back. *Even better.*

"Need help?" Kaleb's smug tone made her wish she could punch *him* in the face. She struck out at the demon instead, hitting him square in the jaw.

The demon grabbed her forearms and pinned her hands over her head. "Humans." He spat the word as if it was blasphemous to admit their race existed. His sour breath nearly gaged her. "So easy to sway, so easy to defeat."

In a show of escape, she struggled, and he clasped both wrists in one clawed grip. He traced the swell of her bosom with a jagged fingernail. She shuddered for his benefit. "No, please . . ."

Eyes glowing deep red, he licked his lips at the sight of her exposed flesh. One sharp nail traced a path from her throat, between her breasts to her navel, a thin trail of blood following in its wake. "I should make you scream for me."

"Kayla," Kaleb warned.

"Oh, for the love of . . ." She muttered an expletive under her breath and banged one heel against the ground, releasing the knife blade resting in the toe of her boot. She kicked upward, bashing the blade into the back of the demon's skull. Blood gushed out onto her leg.

"Ew," she mumbled. *I'm so going to need a shower after this.*

The demon howled, his head lifting to the sky as he let go of her and wrapped his claws around the broken bone and flesh.

Kayla expertly placed her hands on his chest. Summoning all of her Light, she let the energy flow from her fingertips. The demon writhed in pain as his body began to glow redder than hot coals on a barbecue. In the next second, he collapsed into a cloud of ash, leaving Kayla on the ground, her chest heaving from the effort exerted.

Shaking, she propped herself up to a sitting position, coughing as grey dust floated around her, settling on her torn clothing. Kaleb eyed her for a second before applauding with slow claps. She rolled her eyes, and let her head fall back to gaze at the moon and inhaled a cautious breath.

Idiot. "I recall you being a lot nicer in my dreams," she snarled.

"Those weren't dreams." Kaleb hovered above her, eyes shifting to her cleavage for a second, then extended a hand.

Oh, no he didn't. A sweet smile graced her lips, and she clasped his hand. His eyes narrowed in suspicion for a moment, but it was too late. When he pulled to help her up, she shoved, throwing him back off balance. She placed a boot on his chest and kicked him back onto his butt.

Kayla jumped to her feet, raising her hands in a ready position.

Kaleb shook his head. "Not bad. Why didn't you display more cunning when fighting that demon?"

Kayla extended a hand to help him up, then thought better of it, and clasped her hands behind her back. "Who says I didn't?"

"You put yourself in a vulnerable position," Kaleb stated, pushing himself to a stand. "He had you pinned to the ground. You could have lost control."

"A matter of opinion," Kayla retorted. She searched the ground for her wayward weapons. After she'd sheathed the knife and dagger, she tapped her heel on the ground again. The metal winked in the moonlight before disappearing into the toe of her boot.

"Yes, it's my opinion." Kaleb once more stood with his arms crossed, pecs bunched together, in a stance that spoke dominating male.

Kayla snorted at his posturing, even though a teeny, tiny part of her femininity enjoyed his maleness. Feigning innocence, she batted her eyes at him. "I'm a female. I use it to my advantage."

"How so?" His eyes narrowed.

Kayla crossed her arms over her chest, bunching her cleavage together, daring him to break eye contact. To his credit, he didn't.

Shifting her weight to one leg, jutting out a hip, she spoke, sarcasm dripping from every word. "I don't believe I owe you an explanation of any sort, but since you asked ever so *politely* . . . I'll tell you." Dropping her arms, she laced her fingers together in front of her, and stood straight like a good student performing a recitation at the front of the class.

"Since I have to get close enough to touch them, and it's far more effective to stick my hands onto their torso to blow them to smithereens, pretending I'm a helpless female makes the demons think I can't defend myself. I inflict a few wounds, make them believe they're getting the upper hand, then—Bam! I win." She stepped toward Kaleb, and poked him in the shoulder, accentuating her next words. "Every. Time."

He shook his head in disbelief. "Your powers are better than that. Your guardians must cringe every time you have to do this."

She shrugged a shoulder. "They aren't fond of my tactics, but I get the job done. They trust me." Her cheeks heated at the lie. Her guardians had told her time and again to use her powers more effectively, but she'd let fear get the better of her. *Admit it.* Not accepting greater control over her energy and wielding it to the max had held her back. Fear of greatness could be just as crippling as not believing in oneself at all.

Noticing Kaleb's studious gaze upon her, she gestured at the pile of ash on the ground, shifting the scrutiny from herself. "What's so special about him? He wasn't any different than any of the others I've had to hunt, and yet," she paused to wave her hands around and use air quotations, "I was told tonight was supposed to be a *big night*."

"It is a big night," Kaleb said.

"Yeah, well, so far I need a shower . . . yuck," she commented, swiping a palm over the drying blood on her leg then dabbing at the cut on her torso with a fingertip. "And I need some food, and to check my bank account to see if I have enough money to buy a new shirt." She stared down at her chest, lamenting the torn leather. *This was my favorite.* Leather cost a fortune, and she didn't know if she had enough of the monthly stipend from her guardians to cover new clothing.

"You know a plain T-shirt would suffice," Kaleb grumbled. "And it's far cheaper."

"Says you, Mr. Not-Tall-Dark-or-Handsome." Her heart pinged in her chest at the tiny lie. *So, he's a little handsome. It's not like I get good looking men showing up out of the blue every day.* Swearing she heard a cosmic chuckle at her grudging capitulation, she planted her hands on her hips. "And I don't recall asking for an opinion on my attire."

"Just saying."

"Well, don't." She released a sigh. "I don't know why my assignment sent me here tonight."

Kaleb put a fingertip to his lips. "Ssshhh… Listen."

Kayla squinted, as if the action would sharpen sound. "What?"

Kaleb twirled a finger, indicating the air around them. "The presences. Do you feel them?"

The air thickened around her, and Kayla had the sensation she was being watched. "Are we being studied?"

"Probably."

"Huh…Interesting." The full moon chose to shine in all its glory at that moment. Kayla looked up into the night sky, soaking up the moonbeams, the pull of the solstice calling to her soul. "All this has been fun, but I gotta go."

"I'm coming with you," Kaleb said, his tone brooking no argument.

One eyebrow rose in suspicion. "Uh, why?"

"Because you are mine."

Chapter Two

"Excuse me?" Kayla dismissed his claim with a wave of her hand. "I'm yours? I don't think so, pal."

Kaleb couldn't blame Kayla's skepticism. Even he thought insanity had overtaken his brain. *You are mine?* Where had that come from? Yet, when he paused to examine it, he knew from the depths of his soul, she shared his heart. *Dear Lord and Lady—next thing you know, I'll be writing romantic drivel for the masses.*

He clenched his jaw, gritting out his response. "I meant—you are mine to train. It's my job to take over."

"Oh, the hell it is." Kayla snorted in disdain, squeezing his tense facial muscles with her fingertips. "And you look so happy about it too." Releasing him, she turned on her heel, then stalked away, throwing over her shoulder, "I do fine on my own in case you didn't notice."

Kaleb studied her retreating form as she made her way down the walk to the entrance of the cemetery. Scuffed boots encased shapely legs. A firm butt showcased in a short skirt, and lithe shoulders supported by a strong back. Long, dark hair flowed down her back, a few snarls visible in the moonlight that bathed her and the path she walked on. As if sensing her eyes on him, the sway of her hips increased, and she tossed her hair over one shoulder.

Stubborn, sassy woman.

He frowned. *Like I should talk.* This arrangement didn't make him happy either. Their first meeting in person hadn't gone as he'd imagined. *What had I imagined?* He hadn't put any effort into coming up with a way to properly introduce himself, or how to explain they now had to work together.

Kayla thought he'd only been a dream, even though she'd recognized him. As a Walker-Between-Realms, he could visit with people in the ethers, and travel through the veil and back, oftentimes too easily. Once or twice he'd almost gotten lost and not returned to this plane of existence. But Kayla's presence here had grounded him, and always guided him back.

Or so he'd been told. His guardians had warned him about traveling too much, but he enjoyed gathering information, bringing back useful tidbits that helped him in his training to fight demons in this plane. More times than he could count, his guardians had lectured him on the possible dangers of passing between realms. He didn't listen. Despite their protests, he'd honed his skills as a Walker-Between-Realms. They'd shake their heads, thanking the Universe his twin soul kept him here.

Speaking of which... He closed his eyes for a moment, drawing breath deep into his lungs. *Odd.* For so long, he'd felt alone, now with Kayla's physical presence, his weary heart beat a contented rhythm in his chest.

Kaleb opened his eyes to see Kayla exiting the cemetery, taking a left down the deserted sidewalk. *Why doesn't she shift back to her abode? Would be faster than walking.* Closing his eyes once more, he focused inward, reaching out to her with his energy.

"I'll be damned," he muttered, opening his eyes. Her ability to travel between realms lay dormant inside of her. *Why has she forgotten so much?* Another thing he'd have to teach her.

Kaleb broke into a run to catch up to her, urging his brain to find the right words to make her understand. He caught up to her, laid a hand on her shoulder, and spun her toward him. "Don't you remember when we were kids?" His style of abruptness and to the point questions took precedence over eloquence.

"What?" Fixing her eyes on his, her brows drew together.

Kaleb stared into her eyes—hazel eyes he'd seen too many times to count. Memories flooded his consciousness—past lives they'd shared, their visits between realms in this life, the two of them playing as children. *Remember!*

Tentative, her fingertips brushed his jaw, curiosity etched on her features. Her brunette locks fell about her shoulders, and without thinking, he fingered a few strands between thumb and forefinger. *So soft. It's a different color now.*

She shook her head, straightened her spine, and batted his hand away. "How did you do that?"

Confused at her question, he asked, "Do what?"

"Talk into my head."

You can do it too.

What?

See. He raised an eyebrow. *Told ya so.*

Her eyes widened in understanding, then she shook her head. "Okay, what about the other thing?"

"What other thing?"

Kayla gestured wildly. "Before the demon appeared, I heard the signature sound. You made the same sound before you appeared. It's why I thought I had to fight two of them. I didn't expect *your* presence."

He noticed her body tense and couldn't blame her wariness. Shoving his hands into his pockets, he took on a relaxed posture. "I have special skills. You do too. I can teach you."

Her eyebrows inched higher. "Special skills?"

He supposed a more lengthy explanation wouldn't hurt. "I can phase shift. Demons don't suspect my presence in their midst until it's too late."

"Meaning?"

By way of answer, he stared deep into her eyes, willing her to remember all of the powers she possessed.

She took a wary step back, wagging a finger in his direction. "You mean you manipulate your energy to transport yourself from one place to another? And the sound?"

"Parlor trick." He shrugged, going for nonchalant, even though he thoroughly enjoyed doing what most people considered impossible. As a small child, he could transport with ease. Being open to the universe along with one's gifts, helped an immense amount.

What became more difficult as he aged was learning to control it, so he didn't get distracted and end up phasing back into existence with half of his body wedged in an object.

Once he'd allowed his spirit to take a quick visit to another galaxy, while waiting in an amusement park line. Upon his return, he ended up with his leg stuck between a barrier and a mechanism on a carnival ride. His guardians, Dawn Winters and Trey Moon, had rescued him, along with casting forgetfulness spells on the waiting patrons to curb the pandemonium.

Since transporting was one of the ways he and Kayla visited each other, he'd had to learn to keep focused in order to return to his own space in this time. Kayla had other gifts to develop, and over time their visits had become far and fewer in between. He supposed this could be the reason she'd forgotten about it.

For the past ten years, they'd only visited in dreams when Kayla was open to the experience and could return to her body with ease. The time had come for them to learn from each other, to assist the other in developing skills they'd forgotten. According to his guardians, Kayla had a few keys to his locks.

"Parlor trick indeed, that's seriously freaky," she remarked.

Unsure of whether or not she'd read his thoughts, he insisted, "You can do it, too." He rested his palm against her cheek, stared into her eyes, and said, "Remember."

Kayla raised a hand to strike out at him again, then tensed, and froze. "I can—"

"Yes, you can." His tone gentled. "But you've forgotten how." He dropped his hand and pursed his lips together, pondering how to explain. "The dreams we share aren't exactly dreams. Our spirits visit each other, when you are most open to it, which is usually when you're resting or meditating."

She grabbed hold of his hand and stared at the space where his heart beat in his chest. "Oh my god..." Her voice trailed off. "I remember." Her eyes shifted quickly back and forth from his chest to his face, then her hand fell to her side. "Wow."

"Yeah." He scratched at his temple, an awkward silence filling the warm air between them.

"Our promise by the creek?" she whispered.

"I promised to fight alongside you, and I always keep my promises."

"And you...?" Eyes wide, Kayla stared at him.

He nodded in understanding of the three words she feared to speak.

Kayla resumed walking down the sidewalk through the quiet neighborhood, albeit at a much slower pace. The odd porch light cast a glow to light along their way, but for the most part, all human beings appeared to be deep in slumber.

"You promised too," he pressed, confidence faltering.

"I know," she responded, her tone taking on an absentminded quality. .

Frowning, he followed, anxiety niggling at his subconscious. He hadn't expected her utter surprise at his presence tonight. *The only warning she got was that tonight was a special night? Nice one, Universe.*

Kaleb kept pace with her, remaining silent as he attempted to consider the circumstances her point of view.

From the thought projection energy swirling around her, he concluded she'd figured out that what had transpired between them had only been a dream. Even though she had accepted her role in bringing Love and Light into the world, and learned to fight with him, he read the energy and learned her mind had convinced her she'd conjured him as a memory. *I suppose I can't blame her. Sharing the spirit realm with someone is vastly different from sharing physical space. Maybe something happened to make her forget.*

Kaleb scrubbed a hand over his jaw, a five o'clock shadow grating against his fingertips. He hated shaving, yet he chose to keep his bald pate and smooth chin.

"The whole Buddha thing is very apropos. But a goatee would look good."

Startled, he glanced over at her. "Pardon?"

Scowling, she gestured at his head. "Your thoughts are loud. You hate shaving, yet you keep your appearance thusly." Eyeing him for a second, she commented, "I'm not usually into bald guys, but you are kinda cute."

"Back at ya. Cute that is, not bald." He made a twirling motion with one hand. "Your thoughts kind of swirl around you in a sparkly mist."

Surprise registered on her face for a second, then she shrugged. "Huh. Interesting."

He couldn't help grinning, which in turn brought forth a smile and a giggle from her.

She clapped a hand over her mouth. "I don't giggle."

"You used to all the time." He nudged her in the ribs with his elbow.

She stuck her tongue out at him and gave him a shove in the shoulder. "You weren't such a jerk in my dreams."

"You've gotten even sassier."

"Yeah, well since you don't seem to be leaving, get used to it."

"I intend to."

Kayla stopped at the end of a short, tree-lined lane that led up to a small house. A croaking frog song echoed around them. The wind whistled through the evergreens. He waved a hand in the direction of her home. "Your place?"

"Uh-huh." Contentment showed in her aura. "It's close to civilization where I can help, but gives me a little space surrounded by nature." She closed her eyes, and he got the impression she was listening to the foliage welcoming her back to her abode. After a moment, her eyes popped open, and fixed on him. "So."

He nodded. "So."

She pointed to the full moon. "Look, I don't have a lot of time. I've got a date with a ritual. Could we get acquainted later?"

"I'll wait." He shrugged, having no intention of going anywhere at the moment.

Confusion drew her brows together. "Wait for what?"

"For you to be done."

She cocked her head at him. "Don't you have your own place?"

"Yep, but I'm supposed to be here."

Kayla rolled her eyes skyward, and he heard her inward sigh loud and clear. "I don't bite," he offered. "Unless that's your thing."

She snorted and gestured for him to follow her up the lane. "Suit yourself."

As he walked beside her, he sent out energetic feelers. A faint hum of magic surrounded them. He knew her powers were significantly greater, and wondered why he couldn't sense more protection around her place. "You know you really should have more wards up to keep out—"

Raising a hand, she cut off his observation. He ran smack dab into an invisible wall. Stunned for a second, he shook his head. *Note to self: Do not voice unwanted opinions.*

"I didn't say it was unwanted." Kayla looked back over her shoulder. "Proving a point."

"Duly noted," he muttered.

"If you are here to tell me how to protect myself," she called back. "Don't bother. I know how." With a snap of her fingers, she lifted the shield, allowing him to continue on.

"I see that," he uttered under his breath. "Doesn't mean you don't need a little improvement. Or help. Or maybe I'm simply learning more about you."

"Learn this." Kayla rounded on him, using her hand like a spear, aiming at his throat.

He blocked her strike, parrying with one of his own. She stepped into him, turning, at the same time aiming an elbow at his ribcage. Kaleb kept contact with her arm, pushing down, and stepping around which resulted in Kayla pinned to his body, her back to his front.

"Damn," she muttered.

Damn indeed. He wasn't here to enjoy her feminine body pressed up against his. *I'm here to take over her training in order to assist my own.*

Kayla wiggled up against him, her butt grinding into his pelvis. "Do you work out regularly?"

Willing his body not to respond, he sighed, and pushed her away from him. "You know I do, just like you. We learned to fight together, and continued training on our own."

A sigh escaped her lips. "I remember."

"Good. It's a start."

Without another word, she led him up the flagstone walk to her front door, waving a hand to instruct her magic to allow them entry. Once inside, she didn't bother with artificial lighting, moving through the small living room with the ease of a woman who knew her space by heart.

Kaleb stubbed his toe on a piece of furniture—an ottoman he suspected by the size and weight. Her snicker told him she'd walked close to it on purpose just to see if he would be able to navigate his way around it. *Fail.*

Kayla stopped in the kitchen, and in the next second, a *snick* echoed in the quiet room. A flame flared to life, and her shadow danced against the wall opposite as she lit a pillar candle set in the middle of the table. With a definitive tap against the counter top, she placed the lighter down. "Stay."

Although he didn't appreciate being treated like a beloved family pet, her command demanded he obey. It didn't stop him from staring at her butt as she sashayed from the room.

"Eyes up, mister." Her voice faded away as she shut her bedroom door with a click.

Busted.

Glancing around the space, he noted the stove and fridge up against one wall, sink and countertop opposite. An island took up the middle of the room. Noises from Kayla's room drifted out to him: Kayla shuffling about her bedroom, the thud of boots hitting the floor, the whisper of clothing being extracted from drawers. *Do not picture her naked, do not picture her naked . . .*

Exhaling a deep sigh, Kaleb studied his surroundings with increased intensity. The tiny house served a dual purpose. The open concept of the living room and kitchen area with view of the front and back entrances meant she could always see trouble coming. Plus it wouldn't be difficult to upkeep such a small space, freeing up her time to train. The bathroom and bedroom off of the kitchen gave a little privacy, something he valued as well. The layout of his home was much the same.

The bedroom door opened. He refused to turn when he heard Kayla exit her room, the bathroom door closing indicating her intentions. At the sound of the water running in the shower, he emptied his mind and counted: *One Mississippi, two Mississippi . . .* He'd already had an eyeful. He didn't need to conjure unwanted images of Kayla unclothed or otherwise.

An image of Kayla standing in the cemetery, shirt gaping open to reveal average, round breasts pushed up by the cups of a sexy, red lace bra, infiltrated his mind.

Lord and Lady help me. At this time, the point of his physical presence in her life did not include a sexual relationship, something he needed to remember. *Like all the time.*

Running a fingertip along the Formica countertop, he took note of the candles scattered about the room, pictures of nature on the walls, and plants situated near windowsills. He wondered if she ever felt lonely, as he did from time to time.

The opening of the door snagged his attention, and he glanced over to see Kayla enter the kitchen, this time clad in a light pink silk robe that hung past her knees, wet hair spilling messily about her shoulders.

They stared at each other for a moment. Then she cleared her throat, and tightened the sash on her robe. "Help yourself if you're hungry," she offered as she flitted about the room, lighting more candles. "Lots of food in the fridge. But get it now because I don't want any artificial light to interfere in my ritual."

"Done," Kaleb assured.

With a nod of thanks, she glided to the back door, taking the lighter with her. At the door, she turned to speak to him again. "And no peeking."

Kaleb stared long after the door had closed behind her. He did not want to imagine what her ritual might entail. Yet, of their own volition, his feet shuffled toward the door, until he could gaze out the window. Flickering lights told him she'd lit more candles, and he saw her shadow floating around in a high hedgerow he assumed had been groomed into a circle.

"Let her do her thing, no need to look, no need to interfere." He paced the small space of the kitchen, pondering food as a distraction. When he heard Kayla's voice chant the sounds he knew by heart, against his command his hand reached for the doorknob, and opened the door.

Hesitant, he stepped out into the night, letting the door swing shut in a quiet arc behind him. He ceased moving when he stood at the entrance to her sanctuary, her nude body silhouetted by moonlight, the sound of her voice echoing in his ears, and the fluid movements of her body mesmerizing him.

Surrendering his will, he added his voice to hers.

Chapter Three

"Get another eyeful?"

Disoriented, Kaleb blinked. His gaze focused on Kayla who tied the sash on her robe.

"No, I don't think so." An uncomfortable flush heated his face, and he cleared his throat. *What am I embarrassed for?* He couldn't remember anything after the moment he'd started chanting along with her.

"I believe you. Just messin' with ya." Kayla sat on a stone bench situated off to one side of the circle of shrubs. She patted the space beside her, an invitation for him to join her.

Tentative, he took a step inside her sanctuary. "I won't bite," she assured him, a hint of a smile twitching her lips. "Unless that's your thing."

Amusement tickled his gut at her using one of his jokes against him. *It's not far from the truth.* He released an inward sigh. *This should be easy. I know my purpose. I know hers.*

"And the Universe has taught you that life is easy?" she questioned.

He squinted at her.

"That, uh, sigh was pretty big. Plus, you thought things between us should be easy. Are you learning lesson number one?"

He laughed at his own folly. "It's going to take some getting used to the fact that I've met someone who can see and hear me as clearly as I can them."

"Ditto. I have a feeling there will be a huge learning curve on both our parts." She eyed him from head to toe, her attraction to him shining loud and clear.

"That's not why I'm here."

"I know that, too." Her voice went soft, and she lowered her gaze to the ground.

"I-I'm sorry," he stuttered. "I-it's not that I don't find you attractive."

"I understand." She nodded and silence fell between them, broken by an intermittent frog song.

"I told you to stay in the house." Her accusatory tone struck him in the heart.

He sighed in defeat. "Once I heard you chanting . . ." His voice faltered, and he cleared his throat. "I felt compelled to join you. You know that chant."

"EL, KA, LEEM, OM." She nodded. "Earth, Fire, Water, Air, or breath . . . consciousness, however you want to spin it."

"Yeah." He clasped his hands together in his lap, eyes fixed on the grass under his booted feet.

Candlelight flickered around them, fireflies added their light, insect shadows danced around the space. "You're lonely, too."

"Sometimes," he admitted.

"I understand that." Her hands settled in her lap. "Everything I thought was a dream . . . isn't." A statement, not a question. "The training, playing by the creek where we promised to fight together, everything I see. All real?"

He nodded, hope blossoming in his heart.

"And you're here to . . ." Her voice trailed away, and she shrugged a shoulder.

"Continue our training, but together. I have keys to unlock powers inside of you, and you have—"

"—keys to your locks." She pressed her palms together between her thighs. "Okay, I get it."

A smile graced his lips. *She's taking this in stride better than I thought she would. But then again, if she's as strong of heart as I remember, then I shouldn't have underestimated her in the first place.* He realized if their roles were reversed, he would have had a much harder time accepting everything the way she had so far.

"What else am I supposed to do?" she asked. "How do we figure out what to do together?"

He chuckled. "I'm not sure. I guess we both have to get used to this."

Kayla glanced heavenward. "Ah, good old Universe—cryptic suggested direction. I need a drink."

Taken aback at her suggestion, he asked, "Do you drink?"

"Ha! I wish."

A hum in the air disturbed their musings.

"Damn," he muttered. "Guess we get to see what we're made of a lot sooner than we thought."

"What?" Panic infused into her voice. "I don't have any weapons."

"You've got everything you need." Kaleb's eyes narrowed as he stood and moved to the opening of the sanctuary. He peered into the night, summoning energy into his palms. Two demons manifested into existence ten feet in front of him.

"How the hell did they get in here? I only lowered my wards enough to let you in, then I reset them." She rounded on him, fixing him with an accusatory glare. "Don't tell me trouble follows wherever you go."

Sheepish, he fought a grin. "Well, not all the time."

"Stay in here. I can protect us." Kayla's voice warbled in worry, accompanied by a magical hum.

Kaleb took a step forward and bumped into an invisible shield. "Drop the shield, Kayla. You were meant to do this." He glanced back at her. Two more pops indicated more party guests. "*We* were meant to do this. It's a test."

Fear shone in her eyes. "You can do this. You have all the weaponry you need inside of yourself." He held out a hand to her. A succession of pops reached his ears. That put the count at near ten now. "Stop conjuring them," he ordered.

"What are you talking about?" she snapped, waving a hand in his direction. "I'm not making these psychos appear!"

"Yes, you are," he replied, his tone gentle yet urgent. "Your fear—Shadow—is manifesting itself as demons. Breathe. Clear your mind. You are stronger than your fears."

Kaleb could hear Kayla pondering his statement. He knew she'd had to fight her own personal demons during training. In order to defeat evil in the world, a warrior first had to go deep inside and slay their personal demons. Her face took on a look of determination. *Atta girl. You're gettin' it.*

A loud pop resounded. *Oh shit.* Some personal demons needed repeated slaying before they were banished for good.

Kayla's eyes went wide. "I didn't do that! I did what you said."

"I know," he mumbled. "That one's mine."

Kayla peered around him. "When you manifest your fear, it's huge. That's the biggest, ugliest son of a—"

"Kayla—"

"—I've ever seen."

Kaleb swallowed hard, breathing in deep, exhaling slow. He stuck his hand out further in her direction. "Take my hand. You can do this. I'm here to help you. Trust me. We'll defeat them together."

Kayla slowly curled her fingers around his palm. "How do we know which ones are real?"

"It doesn't matter," he insisted, infusing a confidence into his tone he didn't feel. "They all need to be vanquished."

"What am I supposed to do?"

"Same thing you always do," Kaleb said. "Manipulate your energy with your hands."

"But I usually touch them before I summon it to destroy them." She glanced sideways at him. "A quick tutorial please?"

"Something like this." Kaleb snapped his other hand forward, brandishing a whip of Light. The tip struck one of the demons square in the chest. He then concentrated a burst of energy from his fingertips. It traveled down the strand of light, gathering in his opponent's torso. Within seconds, the demon disappeared in a pile of ash. The remainder of the pack snarled in response, teeth dripping saliva, eyes glowing red.

"Cool," Kayla said, awe in her voice.

"You can do it too," he assured her. "Concentrate. Envision what you want to happen, and then do it. Now drop the shield."

He heard her sharp intake of breath, and felt the energy field around them slide into the breeze. "Whatever you say, boss."

"Let's go, girl."

With a sharp nod of her head, she released his hand. Sparks surrounded her as she summoned her Light. Pride shot through him to have her standing at his side.

They stepped out of the sanctuary in sync. The demons advanced.

Kaleb gathered energy into his palms and whipped out two beams of light, hitting two demons, reducing them to ash.

Beside him, Kayla did the same, but used her Light energy as a lasso, wrapping one tendril of light around a demon's neck, and another around his wrist, drawing him closer to her. She released one beam, then lifted her hand palm up and shot an energy ball at his chest. Kayla one, demon zero.

Impressive.

"Thanks. I'm a quick learner," she responded, reading his mind.

"Thank the Lord and Lady," he muttered.

"Not the time to be a jerk," she threw back.

Within a few minutes, grey dust coated the dewy grass. Only one big, bad demon remained.

As he advanced on the pair, Kayla cast a worried glance at Kaleb. "You got this?"

"Yeah." Even to his own ears, he didn't sound convincing.

Out of the corner of his eye, he could see Kayla's gaze fixed on him. *You can do this. Show her how it's done. Then she'll have confidence in training with you.* Once during training, he'd nearly been defeated by this particular personal demon. If not for the help of his guardians, he would have been reduced to curling up in a ball and crying in a corner. Not exactly brave warrior material. He couldn't let his fear get the better of him, especially at a time like this. Not with Kayla watching his every move.

Kaleb released an energy strand from his palm that struck the demon in the shoulder. The glancing blow didn't slow the demon one bit.

Brow furrowing, Kaleb tried again, this time wrapping his energy around the neck of his opponent. Locked in a stand-still, he tried forcing more Light from his body, but it stuck, refusing to manipulate to his will.

Crap. Why would his power falter? *Damn it! Come on.* He could do this. He'd been battling alone for years now. This demon should be a piece of cake.

An energy ball hit the demon in the forehead, startling Kaleb out of his ruminations. Another hit the bad guy's midriff. The demon howled, but held his ground.

"Stubborn son of a gun, aren't ya?" Kayla called out from beside him.

Is she talking about me, or him?

"Both," she replied, once again reading his mind. Rubbing her palms together, she pulled her hands apart, creating an energy web between them. With slow steps, she walked toward the demon.

"Kayla, I got this," Kaleb said, determined to be the victor of the situation.

"Hold him!" she commanded. "Let me help."

Kaleb beat back the conflicting emotions. He knew he could do this alone, yet he understood they had to fight together. The sight of her closing the distance between her and harm, didn't lesson his anxiety. Sure, they'd trained together, bumps and bruises were part of the deal. But now she could get hurt for real. *We both could.*

"Kaleb!"

Kayla's bark brought him back to attention. *Get a grip. She can do this. We both can.* They had a much better chance of winning if he changed his position.

As quick as he could, he retracted his energy, then phased out, reappearing behind their adversary. Mustering his resolve, he whipped out his Light again, wrapping it around his rival's neck and torso. He fortified his Light, anchoring their foe in place.

Kaleb sensed Kayla's anger just as she released a basketball sized burst of energy from her hands. It hit the demon square in the chest where his heart would be if he had one. The force from the reverberating shock caused Kaleb to stumble backward.

Yowza. When she focuses fully on something, does she ever. Heart pounding, Kaleb leaned forward, hands on his thighs, gulping deep breaths of air. The demon's remains added to the ash littering the ground.

The full moon cast an ethereal glow upon Kayla's backyard. The quiet night didn't appear disturbed by the battle they'd fought. As his eyes adjusted to the dim light left in the aftermath, he became aware of Kayla's presence standing in front of him.

Slowly, he straightened to face her, emotions a jumble—pride at how well they worked together, ecstatic that Kayla had risen to the challenge, unease he'd let his anxiety in where it didn't belong, elation they'd won, uncertainty about the future, confusion as to what to do next.

Every emotion must have shown on his face because Kayla wasted no time in confronting him. "Don't ever do that to me again."

Chapter Four

By the crushed look on Kaleb's face, Kayla wished she hadn't voiced her displeasure in such a harsh manner. Blunt being her style; she always got right to the point. Her brand of honesty wasn't always welcome.

"What I mean is," she began, breathing deep to calm her racing heart. "Don't ever disappear on me like that again. I thought we were partners." *Ugh. I sound like a whiny brat.* But the truth was, he had scared her by disappearing.

"I couldn't exactly announce my intentions. It's called the element of surprise." His defensive tone struck at her heart.

She should trust that he wouldn't leave her to battle his demon alone, but at the same time, she didn't know him very well. How could she know what he would or wouldn't do in any given situation? "I suppose." Irritated, she took hold of his elbow and steered him back into the sanctuary toward a bench. "Let's sit for a minute or two. Catch our breath."

Kaleb sat beside her, looking everywhere but at her. They'd just vanquished a backyard full of demons, and he acted as if they'd lost. *But we won!* She studied him for a moment. *Or did we?*

The words whispered into her subconscious, and she took a moment to analyze them. Realization dawned. Tonight hadn't been about her fighting a great battle against evil and winning. It had been about meeting Kaleb, understanding they had a shared destiny, learning to work alongside each other, and accepting that more would be coming their way to face together. *Together.*

She'd never contemplated battling with someone before. Her guardians had been her back up, only interfering if she'd been in trouble. Until tonight, fighting had been a solo exercise. Training prepared a person to fight, but not how to strategize with another—to draw on another's strengths, and fill in the cracks of their weaknesses. *Or have them fill in your own.*

"I could've handled that myself, ya know." Kaleb's mumbled statement held no confidence. Was she supposed to feel bad for helping him out? Hadn't he been the one to say they were to fight together?

Ah, male pride. An old nemesis perhaps? Could she blame him? When he'd showed up at the cemetery, she hadn't wanted his help. A smile twitched the corners of her mouth. How many times had she railed against instructions given to her from the Universe? Kaleb probably didn't fall any farther from the proverbial tree than she did.

"Is this the part where I'm supposed to apologize?" she asked, trying to keep sarcasm from her voice but failing in the most miserable way possible.

"Apologize for what?" he snapped.

"For saving your—" She paused to clear her throat, giving herself a chance to calm her inner fire and amend her statement before she said something out loud she couldn't take back. "For helping you. You did say we'd pledged to fight together, right?"

He nodded in reply.

"We accomplished our task then, correct?" Another nod of his head answered her question. "Then . . ." Her voice trailed off, allowing sufficient time to summon the empathy needed for the question she had to ask. Her hand hovered over his thigh, uncertain of her next move. Since she'd been a child, another gift she possessed—or cursed, depending on the day—was her ability to touch people and know information about them, and often things they tried to hide from themselves.

What's the worst you're gonna find? That he doesn't want to work with you? You're already feeling that, and you can read each other's thoughts. Suck it up, and find out what you need to know, and go from there.

Inhaling a deep breath for courage, she laid a hand on his thigh. "What were you afraid of?"

Kaleb shifted on the spot, obviously uncomfortable under her scrutiny. Her heart went out to him. The ability to empathize with others was another of her gifts she bestowed easily upon others, but not so much on herself. It had been drilled into her from an early age that she was a warrior. She'd taught herself to be strong, tough. She could handle anything alone. Tonight had been the first time she'd truly trusted another individual with her safety. He'd asked for it, and she'd given it. *A big step for me. Why won't he trust me in return?*

Trust is earned, not given.

Kayla closed her eyes, allowing the words sent from the Lord and Lady to penetrate her mind. While she hadn't realized it, Kaleb had earned her trust when he'd appeared for her fight, and insisted she finish what she'd been sent to do. He could've let macho pride take over and shown the "girl" how it's done, but he hadn't, knowing she needed to fight her own battles and ask for help when she deemed it necessary.

Had she blown it? Would he ever trust her now that she'd assisted him in conquering a demon he could have handled on his own? *Maybe I should have stood back and let him fight on his own.*

"I'm sorry."

Kaleb laid a hand over top of hers on his thigh. "You have nothing to be sorry about. We were supposed to work together and we did."

"But . . ." Nibbling her lower lip in worry, she waited for him to further expand his clarification. When none seemed forthcoming, she placed her other hand on top of his. He spread his fingers allowing her to lace their hands together.

"You don't trust me, do you?" she asked, her quiet voice drifting off to blend in with the night sounds.

"It's not that," he said, staring at their joined hands.

"Tell me." By way of encouragement to continue, she gave his hand a squeeze.

After another long moment of silence, he responded. "I didn't trust myself."

Nodding, she urged him to explain.

"I know we have work to do together, and yet I've trained so long on my own. Or sometimes it seems I've done it alone, even though we spent time in between realms together." He gestured between them. "I'm not sure how to do . . . this."

Kayla smiled, her heart opening to him even more. "That makes two of us."

Kaleb fidgeted in his seat. "I've understood for a long time that at some point we would need to meet in person, learn from each other, and figure out our shared destiny. Just now—I became afraid of what it would mean to work with someone. What if I got used to you having my back, and then you couldn't be there? Would I still be able to go it alone?" One leg jiggled in a nervous gesture.

Kayla rubbed a soothing circle on the back of his hand with her thumb. "Even the best of partners don't work together all the time. On occasion everyone has to face something alone. The point is that when we need support, it's there."

A knowing smile lit up Kaleb's face. "I guess I have a little more work to do to conquer my fear then."

Kayla squeezed his hand. "We all have work to do on ourselves. We aren't perfect and we're not meant to be."

"I suppose by trusting you to fight with me," he said. "I've begun to banish my fear of being able to trust another. If I trust in myself to know beyond a shadow of a doubt that you'll have my back when I need it, then I suppose anything is possible."

Kayla smiled, reaching a hand to brush ash off his forehead. "Yeah. Trust is never about someone else—it's about our ability to trust ourselves enough to let the right people into our lives."

"And trusting that another person will know what we need and when."

Kayla's smile faded. "Did I make the wrong call tonight? Should I have let you vanquish that last demon on your own?" Her eyes searched his, and she spoke quickly. "It's just that I figured it was a good chance to work together, combine our powers and see what would happen."

Kaleb cupped the back of her neck, smoothing her hair. "You made the right choice. You didn't judge my fear, only offered to help me with it. It's important for me to accept that."

"I'm glad you see it that way. I thought you might be upset with me for taking over."

He chuckled. "You didn't exactly take over. Besides, I have a feeling you possess a 'take charge' attitude. Something I will need to get used to. And I scared you too with my disappearing act. Trust me, I'll never leave you to fight alone if I can help it."

"I was a little worried." Kayla hung her head, heat suffusing her cheeks. "And yeah, I do tend to take the bull by the horns. Speaking of which, I sense a stubborn streak in you. It appears we'll both have to get used to new things."

A burst of clarity radiated from her heart. Turning her body to face him, she took his hands in hers. *The most important task isn't to battle demons every day and win. Even the ones conjured from our own mind.* She needed to summon her faith, and let someone in, to help her, to assist him, to trust and believe in another individual as much as she believed in herself.

Kaleb tightened his grip on her hand. The act brought forth a memory of running hand in hand through a field of tall grass with him. Other memories flooded her consciousness—the previous lives they'd shared, the training, visits in between realms, all interspersed with memories of her physical existence at home with her guardians.

On instinct, she released one of his hands and held up her left hand between them, palm facing his chest.

A curious expression took over his features, but then understanding dawned in his eyes, and he pressed his hand to hers. Their palms glowed, and she recalled the kiss they had placed in the centre of their hands symbolizing their unconditional love for each other. Love and Light flowed between their fingertips, traveling up their arms until it crossed over their left shoulders and lit up the space over their hearts.

"Please tell me you see that," Kayla whispered.

"Living it right here with ya, girl," Kaleb said, his voice awestruck. After a moment, he chuckled, "Kinda tickles."

A light laugh escaped Kayla's lips, then died out as words long ago uttered in some far off place, infiltrated her consciousness. "Before there were two, there was one—two bodies, one soul, connected by the heart."

A smile took over Kaleb's face. She beamed in return, and laced her fingers through his again. The Light faded until all they felt was the heat of their intertwined hands.

"Well, whatever is in store," she said, "whatever we have to do together or learn—I'm in."

Kaleb pressed his forehead to hers. "Me too."

They stayed that way for a short time, basking in the afterglow of Light still flowing between them.

Kayla stared into his eyes, silent communication passing between them. Intent on training for most of her life, at the age of twenty-five she hadn't had much time for relationships. Traditional romantic entanglements had never been high on her priority list, even though she'd tried dating a couple of guys. Instinct told her that she and Kaleb needed to build a different kind of relationship—a solid foundation built on trust and friendship. *Build a strong bridge, an unbreakable foundation.*

An interesting challenge. She stifled a giggle, and Kaleb's lips twitched at the corners. Finding each other attractive would require a different kind of inner strength to develop their relationship the right way.

A Morning Dove called out to its mate, breaking the spell, and they broke apart. Kayla blinked, noticing dawn's rays brightening the dim skies, stars winking out, vanishing along with the moon.

Kayla stood, smoothing out the front of her robe, displacing grey particles of ash that scattered in the warm pre-dawn air. "Well," she said, expression bright. "I suppose we could start with getting to know each other. After we shower, that is." Kaleb smirked, and she smacked him in the shoulder with the back of her hand. "Smarten up. How about coffee?"

Kaleb placed an arm around her shoulder in a half hug. "Coffee's good."

Arm in arm, they exited the sanctuary. "I'll clean up first, then the bathroom's yours. And you're buying."

"Buying?" he questioned. "You're not making me coffee?"

She shrugged. "Don't have any in the house."

"Why do I have to buy?"

Kayla gave him a shove. "Is chivalry dead? I did save your butt back there."

"You saved *my* butt?" he asked, tone incredulous, elbowing her in the side.

"Calm down, boss," she soothed, poking him in the ribs. At the sound of his chuckle, she rolled her eyes. "Don't get used to that moniker."

"You're the one who keeps saying it," he replied, poking her back. "And don't think I didn't notice the way you liked it when I called you 'girl'."

She shoved him again, attempting to run into the house. "Keep dreaming."

Kaleb caught her about the waist, pulling her into an embrace, peering down into her face. "This is reality." He tucked some hair back behind her ears. "Ya know what's weird?"

Kayla shrugged in response.

"We have the exact same initials."

At that, Kayla rolled her eyes. "*That* is the weirdest part of all this?"

"The Universe does have an interesting sense of humor," he murmured.

"It does indeed." Kayla smiled up at him, and snuggled into his warmth, tucking her head under his chin, wrapping her arms around his waist. "This feels like home. *You* feel like home."

Kaleb squeezed her tight. "Agreed."

"I suppose reality isn't so bad," she mumbled into his chest, wishing she could sleep in his arms for a week.

"A nap does sound like a good idea." Kayla giggled at his mind-reading skills, and he smiled against the top of her head. "And yeah—reality is pretty good."

ABOUT THE AUTHOR

Award-winning author and voice actor **Kellie Kamryn** channels her sweet and sassy side into her romance and poetry writing. A retired elite gymnast and coach who used to give orders in the gym, she spends most of her days being addressed as "Mom". Visit with her at www.kelliekamryn.com

HER SUMMER SURPRISE
By
Karen Sue Burns

Week One: Monday

Rebirth—the perfect word to describe the current state of Maddy Summers: divorced at forty-four, hopeful for the future, and taking a month off from work. It was early June so her CPA practice and her three employees could easily survive without her. She's given them orders not to call her unless blood or fire was involved.

Today was the first day of a remodeling project at her new house. The old house sat on a prime street in the Sweetwater section of Sugar Land, Texas. Professional athletes from Houston's basketball and football teams loved to call the neighborhood home. It hadn't been home to Maddy for over a year. Her ex-husband kept the house while she moved to an apartment until she knew what she wanted. After the completion of the remodeling, she'd have exactly what she wanted.

Her sweet little house on a lazy cul-de-sac was getting a facelift. The doorbell rang and she placed her coffee cup in the kitchen sink. She fisted her hands as she walked to the front door. *Here we go; the beginning of the rest of my life.*

She laughed at the drama queen direction of her thoughts and opened the front door.

"Good morning, Mrs. Summers. I hope you're ready for some dust and commotion." George Goodwin, her contactor for the remodeling project, stood on her porch wearing a tight white tee, faded blue jeans, and work books.

"Good morning to you as well, Mr. Goodwin. And please call me Maddy. I don't think of myself as a Mrs. any longer."

"Will do and you can call me DG."

She frowned and stepped to the side so he could enter. "DG? What does that stand for?"

He walked past her and stood at the entrance to the dining room. "It's Double G for George Goodwin. My dad started calling me that when I was a toddler and it stuck."

"Cute, kids love nicknames," Maggie said as she eyed his bulging biceps and the defined plane of his chest muscles. She drew her gaze back to his face and found him smiling.

"I'd like to go over the schedule for the next four weeks before my guys arrive."

"Let's sit at the kitchen table. Would you like coffee?" She'd never before seen eyes quite like his, intense and very dark. They were the same color as his hair although gray brushed his temples.

"No thanks, I've already had my allotted two cups."

They sat at the small oak table in a corner of the breakfast area. "Please tell me the remodeling won't take longer than three weeks," she said.

"It could take up to four. Is that a problem?"

"When we met before, I wasn't paying attention to the calendar. I have a party planned three weeks from last Saturday."

"Can you change the date if there's a problem?"

"Not really." She debated whether to tell him the truth then decided to lay her cards on the table. "It's the one year anniversary of my divorce being final. I promised myself I'd throw a party to celebrate one year of freedom. I've already sent out the invitations."

He looked at her as a slow grin spread. "I like your style. I will do my best to have the work done in time for your party."

"Great, thank you. You and your wife are officially invited."

He held up his hands, palm out. "I'm not married, don't believe in it. Thanks for the invite, I'll come by myself."

"Feel free to bring a date. Now you have a reason to be done in three weeks."

"I'll do my best for you." He handed her a copy of a spreadsheet. "This is the list of projects and the tentative completion dates. Look it over and we can discuss any questions you have."

She reviewed it and everything they'd earlier talked about was there. The finish date was four weeks minus a day. She'd ignore that as he said he'd do his best to finish the remodeling quicker. He seemed like such a nice man and his references were excellent.

"I think we're good to go with your schedule," she said, excited that day one of the remodel had finally arrived. "I can't wait to get started and then finished."

"The party is still on. My hunky contractor said he'd do his best to finish early." Maddy sat at the bar of the Marriott hotel in Sugar Land with her best friend, Jules. It was almost six o'clock and they were catching up with a glass of wine.

"He's hunky, huh?"

"I didn't say he was hunky."

"You sure did, must have been a Freudian slip. You think your contractor's hot," Jules said in a sing-song voice.

"Do not. Well, maybe a little hot. Okay, he's hot." Maddy could deal with a contractor so easy on the eyes.

"That should make your remodeling project a lot more interesting."

Maddy didn't want to discuss her contractor's hotness. It seemed weird or at least disrespectful.

"They did demolition of my master bath today and dust is everywhere."

"Get used to it. When Jeff and I did our remodel everything was coated in dust for weeks."

"DG said that would be the case and to try to ignore it."

"Oh . . . so you had a conversation about domestic things with your Mr. Hunk." Jules had a hand over her mouth and would be giggling soon.

"Stop it, please. He's not my Mr. Hunk. He's, uh . . . he's my contractor who happens to be easy on the eyes. I hope his work is as good as his looks."

"Surely you got a recommendation before you hired him."

"Actually, three, people like him." Maddy had done her due diligence and felt comfortable she had selected the right man.

"There you go. I bet everything will work out great and be on time."

"I hope so. I really want my party to be on the actual anniversary."

"That reminds me, I saw Roger yesterday. He was at The Lemmon Tree with a model type-blond."

"Male or female?" Maddy couldn't help herself from making a catty remark.

"Ha-ha, female, of course. They had a huge bottle of champagne next to the table."

"See how hard he has to work to get lucky—fancy restaurants and champagne. Poor man, I'm sure being married to me was a bore to him."

"Why do you say that?" Jules was clearly surprised at Maddy's comment.

"Have we not talked about this at least a million times? He didn't have to work with me on anything. I gave in to him like a beach-front condo in a cat-five hurricane."

"You're right. I know you did and it was unlike you. You're an assertive, hard-ass woman at work and I never understood why you kowtowed to Roger."

"Because I'm an idiot and did exactly what my mom did with my dad. She was a door mat for him and I modeled the behavior thinking that's what proper wives do." Maddy pushed her hair behind her ears. Why were they talking about her marriage?

"How did you come to this conclusion? I've never heard you talk about your mother as a wife."

"Therapy," Maddy said matter-of-factly.

"Therapy, you mean with a psychologist?"

"I started a couple months after Roger moved out of the house. Smartest thing I've ever done." Maddy meant that, too. She'd learned so much about herself, including that she had a tendency to give-in to keep from facing a confrontation. She'd demonstrated that time after time with Roger—anything to keep peace in the house.

"I've never been to therapy. Why didn't you tell me you were going?"

"It wasn't because I don't trust you or value your opinion. I wanted to keep it to myself until I felt like I understood my marriage and why it failed—why I failed."

"Oh, honey, you didn't fail, you escaped from a lousy situation," Jules said quietly.

"Nothing is one-sided. I didn't uphold my end of the marriage. It's like a scale with the husband and the wife on opposite ends. They both have to share an equal weight to keep everything balanced and going smoothly."

"Please tell me how you didn't do your share to keep the marriage going."

"A major problem was how much time I spent to build my CPA practice. Many nights I didn't get home until close to ten." Maddy drank her water. Strange that she and Jules had never seriously discussed why her marriage failed.

"Wasn't that a similar schedule for Roger?"

"I should have gotten home earlier and cooked a nice dinner so that Roger would come home to eat rather than going out with one of his co-workers." At this point, Maddy wasn't sure she truly believed her own words about who should have cooked family dinners.

"Seriously? You believe that load of crap? Why didn't he get home early and cook you dinner?"

"That would have been nice, of course. But Roger doesn't know anything about cooking other than uncorking a bottle of wine. It was my responsibility, although the truth is the girls' nanny did most of the cooking."

"You discussed this with your therapist, right?" Jules's words came out fast. "What did she say about you taking credit for everything that went wrong in the marriage?"

"I don't blame myself, not entirely at least, for the dissolution of my marriage. Like I said it takes two to make things work. I should have worked harder on my end. Roger, too." Six months after the last therapy appointment and Maddy could finally admit Roger had been at fault.

"Did your therapist agree with you?"

"Not entirely, that's one of the many topics we discussed."

"What else did you discuss?" Jules fired the question like a prosecuting attorney.

"Geez, what is this, an inquisition?"

"I'm trying to understand why, after months of seeing a therapist, you still have such a lousy attitude about dating, relationships, and marriage."

"I don't have a lousy attitude." Maddy shuddered at how defensive that sounded

"How many dates have you gone on since your divorce was final?"

"I've been busy with my practice and don't have time for men." In fact, Maddy's practice had grown twenty percent in the last year. Thus, the time not spent on dating had been worthwhile.

"Oh, give me a break. You're not at your office 24/7. I remember several calls from you about new recipes you tried. You had time for that."

"A person has to eat."

"Just admit it—you believe you're tarnished or scarred or something and not suitable relationship material. All because of your marriage to Roger, the jerk, who treated you like crap and you still believe the divorce was your fault." Jules crossed her arms over her chest, she had said her piece.

"Is that what I sound like? Like I'm tarnished."

"Honestly . . . yes, that's how you sound."

"Oh."

"But more importantly, is that what you truly think about yourself?"

Maddy remained silent and avoided the question. The truth wasn't that she still believed the divorce was all her fault; the more than two-dozen therapy sessions had been worthwhile. The truth was that she was afraid—afraid to step out into the dating/relationship world. What if she screwed up again? Being a two-time loser at love held far more fear for her than living the rest of her life alone.

Week One: Wednesday

For the last two days Maddy couldn't get her conversation with Jules out of her head. That comingled with prior conversations with her therapist and she was on a virtual merry-go-round that continued to spiral in her head.

Today she'd started refurbishing a rocking chair that had been her grandmother's. It had multiple layers of varnish and she was determined to reach bare wood without the use of chemicals. Thus, the sanding was slow and tedious. She worked on the patio, out of the way of the workmen who building her new master bath walk-in shower. The weather was on the cool side for June so she wasn't too uncomfortable on a Texas summer afternoon.

She'd created so much dust from her sanding that she needed to wipe down the chair. She went inside the house for a rag and ran into DG in the kitchen.

"Hey there, checking on the progress?"

"Yes, ma'am, everything appears to be on schedule."

"That's what I like to hear. They've made good progress on the shower." She couldn't wait for her first shower surrounded by glass.

"We'll start the demo of the floors tomorrow. It's loud."

"No problem, I'll be outside. Let me show you what I'm working on. Would you like iced tea?"

With a glass of tea in one hand and a wet rag in the other, she led DG to the patio. "This is my project during the construction."

"Nice looking rocker."

"It came to me from my grandmother. Her mother received it on her wedding day as a gift from her father. That would be my great-great grandfather, I think." She counted greats on her fingers. "Yeah, that's right."

"That's some history."

Maddy sat in a sling-back chair and motioned for DG to join her in the other. "When I was little, my grandmother and I would sit in the chair and she'd read me stories. I loved to stay at her house when my parents went out."

"My nana lives in an assisted-care facility now but man, could she bake cookies. My favorites were molasses and peanut butter."

"My grandmother's specialty was pies. She loved making the crust and it was flaky and tender." Maddy laughed. "I sound like a TV commercial."

"Nah. What's your favorite pie?"

"Any fruit pie, coconut cream, pecan, and of course, chocolate pie."

"That covers a lot. Do you bake any of her recipes?"

"I've made at least half of them. My ex-husband wasn't a big sweet eater so the baking was for a family gathering or I'd take one to the office."

"You have a big family?" DG stretched out his long legs. She sighed, enjoying the sight of a handsome man relaxing on her patio and sighed. Now, this she could get used to.

"I'm an only child so I don't have a niece or nephew but tons of cousins. Both my parents came from large families."

"That's something we have in common. I'm an only child, too and there are many cousins on both sides of the family. My cousin Chad is my best bud."

"My ex came from a small family and holidays with the whole gang were torture for him. One of the many differences that finally drove us apart." She had a long list of why she and Roger were incompatible.

"I hope I'm not prying, but do you have children?"

"Twin daughters, Erin and Ella. They're students at Texas A&M and taking summer classes after their first year. They have a grand plan to graduate in three years."

"Ambitious," DG said.

"I don't know, we'll see. What about you? Kids? Oh, sorry, you said you aren't married."

"Not married or divorced but I do have a son. He's seventeen and will be a senior at Clements High next year."

"Guess that must be a story."

"You are perceptive," DG said with a chuckle.

"One of my many attributes."

"A girl I dated got pregnant," DG said, his voice resolute. "We didn't like each other enough to get married but both of us wanted to be good parents so things have worked out great over the years."

"The mother lives around here?"

"Two blocks from my house. Trevor switches off between houses every other week. He loves it. Says he gets more stuff that way."

"Leave it to a kid to judge a living arrangement based on stuff." She liked the straight forward manner in which DG talked about his son.

"No kidding, he's a great kid. I'm lucky to have him as my son."

Maddy's heart melted at DG's last comment. How wonderful for a father to think about a child like that.

DG enjoyed talking with Maddy. Not only was she a beautiful woman with her chestnut hair pulled back in a ponytail and her blue eyes glittering in the sun, but she was easy to talk with. She didn't twitter or make silly suggestive comments. He valued a good conversation and seldom ran across that quality in the women he dated. Maybe he'd been looking in all the wrong places for his dates.

But whether or not she could hold her own in a decent discussion wasn't important. He'd continue with his plan to avoid serious entanglements with any woman. His involvement with Trevor's mother had proven to him that he wasn't a long-term relationship type of guy. He was too damned fickle, which Chad mentioned at least once a month.

He'd never before dated a client. It didn't seem proper. But that didn't mean he couldn't see her outside of her house. It would be as friends or more like acquaintances, definitely not a date. He could take her to dinner, or use the tickets Chad had given him. That was a better idea, not as personal.

"You like baseball?"

"Baseball? Sure. I've been to a couple Skeeters' games in the last year."

"How about the Houston Astros?"

"I used to go with my dad all the time."

"Good," he muttered to himself. "I have tickets for the game on Saturday, playing the Yankees. Would you like to go with me?"

"That'll be a good game. My dad loved the Yankees. Sure, sounds fun."

"Great. We can talk details later." He rose and walked to the end of the patio. Being so close to Maddy was getting to him. It had been a long time since he'd had such a strong reaction to a woman. He needed to get his mind and body under control or he'd be making a big fool of himself. The job should be his primary focus as far as Maddy was concerned. He turned to face her.

"Do you mind coming with me to the bath? We need to go over the tile in the shower."

"Of course." Maddy followed him into the house.

Once inside the master bath he pointed to the cement board encasing the new shower walls. "We need to confirm the top height for the tile and the location for the decorative accent tile."

Her eyes narrowed for a moment then she stepped forward onto the base of the shower. She eyed the spot for the shower head and held her hand a few inches above it. "I think this should be the top of the tile. Have the accent between the head and the control valve, about two-thirds up from the valve. Does that work?"

"Yeah, most homeowners aren't so precise."

She laughed. "I'm a CPA, detail is my middle name."

"That's good, makes my job easier. How are you about changing your mind? You know, on colors, tile, cabinets?"

"Ah, I guess you've had a customer or two change their mind. I'm set on what I've picked out so far." She walked past him out of the bathroom and turned back. "Unless it totally sucks."

Week One: Friday

Early Friday morning DG mentioned that demolition of the kitchen would start the next week with two weeks scheduled to finish. Both the refrigerator and the microwave would continue to be operational so Maddy had a list of dishes to prepare and freeze. But right now it was close to five o'clock on a Friday evening and minutes away from happy hour. She slipped a pan of asparagus rolls in the oven.

A few minutes later DG knocked on the back door and walked inside. "Something smells good."

"Making a couple of appetizers."

"You remember the stove and oven will be pulled out on Monday." He stood on the other side of the small island.

"Yes, I remember and I'll be making a couple of casseroles this weekend and stocking up on paper plates." She stirred chopped spinach into a sour cream, mayonnaise mixture.

"Good, don't won't any surprises." He eyed the bowl with the spread. "What are you making there?"

"A spinach spread for pita chips."

"Pita chips?"

She lifted a bag off the counter and shook it. "Pita chips."

"Oh." He scrunched his eyes for a second then turned toward her bedroom. "Better go inspect the work. It's time for the guys to knock off for the day." He disappeared down the hall.

Maddy finished the spread with chopped water chestnuts, and salt and pepper. She popped a spoonful in her mouth, perfect, and glanced at the clock over the stove. Jules should arrive in ten minutes.

She dragged a bottle of cabernet from the pantry. Messina Hof was one of her favorites, the winery being in Bryan, Texas, not too far up the road. After uncorking it, she set it next to a pair of wine glasses. She nodded in approval, things would be ready when Jules arrived.

Two workers strode from the hallway to the back door. They waved at her as they exited but said nothing. A moment later, DG appeared.

"We're done for the week. The shower will be grouted on Monday and the kitchen demo will start. I—"

"Sorry." Maddy help up her hand as her cell phone trilled. "I need to answer this." She turned away from him as she put the phone to her ear.

"I can't make happy hour," Jules purred. "Hubs got tickets to *Wicked* and he's taking me to dinner."

"No problem. Y'all enjoy and let me know how you like the play." Maddy clicked off and stamped her foot on the soon-to-be-replaced ugly tile. "Damn, I can't eat all this myself."

"Everything okay," DG asked.

She turned around, embarrassed at acting like a three year-old in front of him. "It's nothing. My friend was coming over for a glass of wine and now she can't make it."

He placed a hand over is heart. "I'd be happy to try your spinach spread if you need a taste-tester."

She noticed his flirty grin as he offered his services. Why not? The workday was officially over and she had already opened the wine and prepared the appetizers. "Okay. Might as well have a glass of wine, too. It's Messina Hof cabernet."

"One of my favorites." He slid into a bar stool on the other side of the counter.

Maddy handled him a glass of wine and filled a basket with pita chips and placed them with the spinach spread in front of DG. "Try this."

He slathered a chip with the spinach and stuffed it in his mouth. He chewed for a moment. "I like it. I don't often have homemade happy hour food."

"You eat out mostly?" She pulled the asparagus rolls from the oven and scooped the pieces onto a serving plate.

"Sometimes, but I do cook. I have to for Trevor. We use the grill a lot and I can fix a good salad and some vegetables. Nothing fancy though."

"Sounds like Trevor has a good dad." She placed the plate on the counter. "Try these. My girls love them."

He popped a roll in his mouth and smiled. "Are these hard to make? Maybe I could cook them for Trevor sometime."

"They're easy to make. I'll write out the recipe for you." Maddy sipped her wine then retrieved a note card and a pen from a drawer. "I just realized something. I need to empty all the cabinets and drawers in here."

"My guys can do it for you."

"No, I'd rather do it myself."

"Boxes and tape are in the garage. Stack what you pack in the dining room and we'll move everything to the garage on Monday."

She nodded. "I'll get it done. I won't do anything to slow down the work. My party is two weeks from tomorrow."

"We're on schedule." DG continued to eat the appetizers. Maddy appreciated a man who liked her cooking, even if it was only snacks.

"I'm also giving you the recipe for a chicken-broccoli casserole that my girls love." She wrote out both recipes as they sipped wine and munched. Usually she became uncomfortable when the conversation stagnated—but the pleasant silence with DG made for a nice change. She placed both cards on the counter.

"Here you go. I hope Trevor likes them."

"He'll be with me next week so I'll try the casserole." He chuckled to himself.

"What's so funny?"

"I tried to bake a cake once, chocolate, from one of those mixes. I thought I'd done it correctly but when Trevor cut into it was hard."

"Missed an ingredient?"

"The oil and a second egg." He rubbed a hand over his face. "Pretty sad that a contractor can't follow directions on a cake box. I have orders from Trevor never to try baking again."

"Lucky for you we have plenty of bakeries in Sugar Land," she teased as she topped off their wine glasses.

"True. Your girls give you a hard time about anything?"

"Where to start?"

"That bad?"

"Girls are different from boys as teenagers, much more dramatic. They're good kids but they definitely kept me on my toes. We had a live-in nanny until their senior year in high school who kept things on an even keel."

Surprise registered on his face. "A nanny? I don't know anyone who has a live-in nanny."

"Not my idea. Roger insisted on one if I wanted to work. We both worked long hours so it turned out for the best."

"Did your girls look to the nanny as a parent more than you and their father?"

"That's something I was initially concerned about since Maria spent more hours with them than me. But they know the difference between mommy and the nanny. She was like a favorite aunt in the family. We all loved her."

"Glad it worked out for you, seems weird though. Trevor's mother works but never has any help at the house other than a cleaning lady."

Maddy didn't like to be compared to another mother, especially someone she didn't know. "Every family has a different situation. Not everyone can afford a live-in worker in the home."

"Sure . . . right." He rose and drained his wine glass. "I better get going. It's been a long day."

"Of course." She walked around the counter and headed to the front door.

"Thanks for the wine and snacks." He held up the cards, "And the recipes. I'll try the casserole on Sunday."

"I hope Trevor likes it."

"I'll pick you up at six for the Astros game tomorrow." He walked to his truck and waved after he backed out of the driveway.

Maddy had considered cancelling but now it would be awkward. "Okay, see you tomorrow. Good night." She waved then shut the door.

She returned to the kitchen and washed the wine glasses while debating whether or not to beg off from the game. Was it a smart idea to see her contractor on a social basis when she hardly knew anything about him? If there was a major problem on the remodel, a personal relationship would impact how she handled it. Would she give in too easily or not stand her ground if they disagreed? She couldn't take the chance.

DG was too attractive.

The Astros game would be the one and only event she would attend with him.

Week One: Saturday

DG carried a paper tray holding two beers, two hotdogs, a large bag of peanuts, and two candy bars—the baseball dinner of champions. The Astros-Yankees game was in the bottom of the second inning as he plopped into the seat next to Maddy.

"Here's a beer and a hotdog." He stowed the tray under his seat.

"Nothing happened while you were gone, still double-zip."

"The night is young."

"Oh, yeah." Maddy smiled at him and raised her beer in salute.

The evening with Maddy seemed to be going okay. Last night had gotten weird talking about the nanny. He wouldn't make that mistake again—no asking anything about her life when she was married. He had a hunch her ex-husband was a real douchebag.

They inhaled their hotdogs watching the game. Neither team could get a hit so the innings were short. DG reached under his seat, grabbed the bag of peanuts, and opened it.

"This is our next course, m'lady." He offered the bag to Maddy.

"Thank you, kind sir." She scooped out a good supply of peanuts onto her lap. "I do love nuts."

"Good to know."

She glanced at him out of the corner of her eye. "Right."

The game continued at a slow pace. Neither team could connect a ball with a bat. Finally, the seventh inning stretch came and they stood, grinning at each other and shrugging their shoulders.

"Sorry I didn't bring you to a more exciting game." DG put an arm around her waist and hugged her. "I promise the next one will be more exciting."

"No problem," Maddy said. "It's not your fault the Astros can't get a hit."

In the eighth inning the Astros finally connected for a homerun. That must have invigorated the team as the next two batters also scored.

DG absentmindedly patted Maddy's knee. "Now we're cooking."

The batter up hit a high foul ball that headed right for them. DG watched it angle toward them, as if in slow motion. "Here it comes."

Maddy stretched her hands out in front of her to catch it. The ball hit her left hand then bounced off an arm rest to land somewhere behind them.

"Oh crap, that hurts," she cried, hugging her hand to her stomach. "I think it broke my thumb."

DG placed a hand gently on her arm. "Let me see." She raised her hand and he examined it, sucking in his breath. The thumb was crooked and starting to swell.

"Dude, looks like she broke her hand, better go to the ER." A guy sitting behind them offered his opinion.

DG ignored the comment. "I think we better leave. Here let me help you get up. Don't use your hand for anything."

Maddy answered with a shaky "Okay."

Determined to get this situation fixed, DG helped her up the long flight of steps to the concourse. "Let's take the elevator down. It'll be quicker."

She let him lead her off, all the while clutching her hand to her stomach. "It really hurts. You have any pain relievers on you?"

"No, but I'm taking you to a hospital."

"I don't need a hospital. There's an emergency care center not far from my house. They can do an x-ray and it's a lot cheaper than an ER."

"Whatever you say." He kept his hand on her back as they exited the elevator and made their way to the parking garage. What a lousy thing to happen. Poor Maddy was acting like a trooper as he knew it must hurt like hell. Her face had grown pale, and lines around her mouth told him she was fighting the pain.

He rubbed her shoulder. "Hang in there. It won't take more than twenty minutes to get to the care center."

She nodded, her lips tightening into a thin line—a sure sign she was hurting.

"Thanks for stopping at the pharmacy." Maddy handed her house key to DG to let them in the front door. The visit to the emergency care center was fairly quick for a Saturday night. She had a sprained thumb and would need to wear a splint for three to four weeks. She needed to ice it for the next few hours and take an anti-inflammatory drug. It could have been much worse.

They went to the kitchen for ice.

"I see you made progress today in clearing out your cabinets," DG said as he surveyed the boxes in the dining room.

"Glad I did that much."

"I can help you finish."

"No need. I'll call Jules in the morning. She can come over for an hour and we'll be done." Maddy selected a bag of frozen corn to ice down her hand.

"That corn will work. What can I do for you before I go? Need something to drink, eat . . . anything?"

She grinned and shook her head. "I'm fine. But thanks for asking."

"I'll head out then." He stepped toward her and leaned closer. "Get some sleep."

He was so close Maddy could see flecks of gold in his brown eyes. His citrus scented cologne swirled around her. He stroked her cheek with a finger then gently kissed her. "I'll see you around eight Monday morning. Call me if you need anything." He stepped back and smiled. "I really am sorry about your thumb."

If took her a moment to concentrate on his words as she was still wrapped up in the touch of his lips. "Uh . . . sure. It wasn't your fault."

"Keep it iced." He backed his way slowly to the door. "Good night, I enjoyed the game."

Still holding the bag of corn over her hand Maddy watched him walk to his truck and climb in. She shut the door with her hip and leaned her back against it.

"What the hell just happened? He kissed me and I liked it."

Week Two: Monday

Monday morning came much too soon for Maddy. She was sore from all the kitchen packing on Sunday and had said to hell with icing down her hand. She'd deal with it. As soon as she'd poured a cup of coffee she heard the back door open. She'd already opened the garage door.

"Hello," DG said as walked in. "Good morning, how's your thumb?" He stopped on the other side of the island.

She raised her hand. "All good, doesn't hurt that much and the swelling is better. Would you like coffee?"

"No thanks. Glad it's doing well." He walked around the island. "Everything out of the cabinets and drawers?"

"Yes sir, I'm ready for the demolition. I packed a kitchen bag so I won't starve." She pointed to boxes along a wall of the breakfast area.

"No problem, we'll move them. It'll get noisy so hide out in another room."

Two of the workers walked in and waited by the door for instructions from DG.

"I'll be in the bedroom reading. Holler if you need me." She took the coffee mug with her and went to the guest bedroom, shut the door, and plopped on the bed.

She turned the television to a cable news show and opened a book, a contemporary romance that was sure to keep her mind off the noise.

Thirty minutes later they started on the demo based on the noise level. The cabinets would be demoed first, then the floor with a jackhammer. She concentrated on reading Jake and Eileen's love story, ignoring the demise of her kitchen. In two short weeks she'd have the kitchen of her dreams, or at least the kitchen of her budget.

She dozed off after a bit and woke with a jerk. Panic coursed through as her gaze darted to the clock on the bedside table. Whew, she wasn't late for lunch but she needed to hurry. She ran her fingers through her hair and gathered her purse and keys.

She waved at the guys in the kitchen. "I'll be gone for a couple of hours."

Within ten minutes she pulled into the parking lot of Lupe Enchilada, a Mexican restaurant that had been in Sugar Land for many years. She'd always loved it, but the fact that Roger had hated it was an even bigger draw for her these days.

She walked in the tall wooden door held open by a cute greeter and spotted Jules just inside. She turned and her eyes zeroed in on Maddy's hand.

"What happened to you?"

"I'll tell you once we're seated."

They were ushered to a booth in the section of their favorite waiter, Jessie, a teenager going on forty who attended the local community college. She arrived immediately.

"Hey y'all, how's it going?"

"Just fine, Jessie," Jules said. "I'll have a glass of ice tea and my usual taco salad."

"Same here," Maddy said. "How's summer school?"

"Eyeball deep in finals now, and then I'll have a month off." She pumped her fist then walked away to place the order.

Once Jessie left, Jules leaned over the table, concern painting her face. "Are you okay? Why didn't you call me?"

"Hold on. It's no big deal. At the baseball game I tried to catch a foul ball and it hit my thumb. It's just a sprain so I have to wear the splint for a bit."

"Wait. Who'd you go to a baseball game with?"

"DG. He got tickets from his cousin and I used to go with my dad so I decided to go with him. In fact, I—"

"Hold on." Jules raised a hand in front of her chest like a traffic cop. "Let me get this straight. You had a date with your contractor?"

"No. No, it wasn't a date. We just went to the game together."

"Did he pick you up?"

"Yes."

"Did he buy you food like say, beer and peanuts?"

"Yes."

"Did he take you—"

Perturbed with her line of questioning, Maddy interrupted Jules. "Oh, stop it. It wasn't a date."

"Then what was it?" Humor spread across Jules's face. She loved this conversation.

"Two new friends enjoying a fun event together, that's all. I'll invite him to something to pay him back."

"Like what?"

"Like I don't know. Let me think."

Jessie arrived with the tea so Maddy had a reprieve from providing an idea. She had no clue what to invite DG to anyway. She hardly went anywhere unless it was a CPA training workshop. In fact she had one at the end of the week in San Antonio.

She attempted to change the subject. "How was the play?"

Jules leaned back against the booth's cushion. "It was wonderful. I loved the music and the costumes were so colorful. Jeff enjoyed it but you know he has a hard time sitting that long."

"Maybe we should look into getting season tickets this year. Houston has so much to offer for plays and musicals."

"Good idea. I'll check into it," Jules replied.

Jessie served their salads. "Enjoy, ladies."

"What's happening with the remodeling?" Jules asked as she poked her fork in her salad and sifted through the lettuce.

"You know the green stuff is healthy," Maddy said with a glint of humor.

"I know. I like to eat the good stuff first."

"Anyway, the remodeling is moving right along. They're demolishing my kitchen today. I'm so happy this part of the job has started." Maddy nearly bounced in her chair. "Soon I'll have a gas stove."

"That must be exciting," Jules said sweetly.

"Also, everything is still on schedule so the anniversary party date won't change. Glad I sent out the invitations."

"Do you need help with the food?"

"I'll handle most of it, but I'd love a bowl of your potato salad. It's always a hit." Maddy figured Jules would offer to help. She could always count on her friend.

"I will bring it along with my walnut brownies."

"Great idea, thanks."

"My pleasure. Now . . . tell me about the baseball game. What was hotter . . . the dogs or DG?"

Week Two: Wednesday

Maddy passed the cooler Tuesday morning hours sanding the rocking chair and the warmer afternoon in the guest bedroom, reading. She had many projects to complete but any work was impossible with her house in the middle of chaos. The floor tile installers laid the slate-looking porcelain tile in her bedroom and bath.

Completion of the grout work on Wednesday meant her furniture could be moved back in, the first step of her house getting back to normal.

DG arrived late-afternoon to inspect the section of floor that was finished. Maddy was happy with it but understood the installers relied on DG for final approval. After all, he had hired them.

She sat on the patio while he made his inspection. The rocking chair had one more session of sanding that she'd do once everyone left. She was slower now with the splint on her hand. Having so many people in and out of her house during the day was getting to her. Just that morning, she'd gathered the multitude of empty drink cans and told one of the workers to take his belongings home.

DG opened the patio door and joined her. "Good news, we can move your bedroom furniture back."

"That's what I was hoping. The floor looks really good. I'm pleased with the tile I selected."

"It does look good. Do you want everything in your bedroom in the same location?"

"Yes. Do I need to show you?"

"No, the guys did a sketch. I'll come back when they're done so you can check it out."

She nodded as he turned to go back in the house. So far the remodel had progressed smoothly and without a problem. That couldn't be normal. Nothing involving this much money, detail, and time could go too long without a hiccup. She was a realist and knew it was just around the corner.

She read her romance novel under the umbrella, working at staying cool in the middle of summer.

Eventually dark clouds scurried in along with the wind. The palm fronds along the fence were dancing and the wind chimes played a lilting song. She rose, folded up the umbrella, and went inside to find everyone putting the finishing touches to her bedroom.

The workers smiled on their way out the door, their workday over. Only DG remained and he turned to her. "Anything I need to move?"

She checked the location of the headboard, verified it was centered properly, and the armoire was also in the correct spot. "Looks good, I can sleep in my own bed tonight." She walked into the bathroom, surveying the updated space. "And use my new shower. This will be fun and luxurious."

"Taking a bath alone in that big walk-in shower is fun?" DG was right behind her, grinning like he had hit the lottery.

"Ha-ha. I'll enjoy every moment pretending I'm at some fancy spa." She made a silly face, inciting them both into a fit of laughing.

"Anyone ever told you that you have a good sense of humor?" DG commented. "You're a lot of fun."

"That's me, the comedian CPA. And that which reminds me, I'll be away from the house starting at noon tomorrow and then return on Saturday. I need to go to a training seminar."

"Won't be a problem. I have a key and will make sure the house is locked tight after the guys leave Thursday and Friday evenings."

"Good. I know you're bonded so if anything should happen, it's covered."

"Don't worry about a thing, enjoy your seminar." He walked out of the bathroom then turned back to her. "By the way, I made your casserole last night. Trevor said it was quote-unquote 'tasty' which is a big complement from him."

"Good for you. I'll go through my recipe box for other casseroles that are easy and quote-unquote tasty."

"Thanks. I'll head out now."

They stalled at the front door. The wind was blowing so hard the rain fell horizontally. The gutter on the corner of the house flowed like Niagara Falls. This storm was staying put for a while.

"You shouldn't be driving in that wind. Looks like you're stuck with me for a bit." Maddy shrugged her shoulders. "Want a glass of wine? We can watch the storm from the kitchen."

His gaze narrowed at the empty space.

"I told you I'd be prepared." She grinned at him. "Hold on, I'll be right back."

DG rubbed a hand over the stubble on his jaw. Maddy was sure something else. She was probably one of those women who had everything in her handbag, prepared for every emergency. He smiled at that image in his head. Noticing they had no place to sit, he went to the garage to forage for chairs.

He walked back in the house with two folding lawn chairs and found Maddy holding two glasses of wine.

"I had to pour them in the bathroom," she said. "Good idea about the chairs. We can watch the rain."

He opened them and set them by the large kitchen window facing the patio and backyard. "Have a seat." He accepted and glass of wine and held the back of a chair while Maddy sat down.

"Isn't this the life?" she said, holding her glass in front of her. "Drinking wine, sitting on bare foundation in a lawn chair, and watching Mother Nature storm." She tapped her glass against his. "Life doesn't get much better than this."

"Although . . . it would be nice sitting under clear blue skies on a white beach somewhere."

She nodded, "There is that."

The more time DG spent with Maddy the more he liked her. He snuck a glance at her as she watched the rain. She was so pretty and so, well, spunky. Yeah, that was the right word—spunky. But she also had that little extra something he found damn attractive in a woman. He couldn't find the right words to describe it. Didn't matter if he could put a name to it or not, she had it. And he liked it.

"Something wrong?" she said, looking down. "Did I spill wine on my shirt?"

She had caught him staring at her. "No, I was just thinking."

"Thinking about what?"

"Nothing." God, he sounded lame.

"Okay." She gave him a sideways look.

He felt like a freaked out teenager on his first date. But this wasn't a date and his teenage days were long past. He was sitting with a client and not a woman he could legitimately flirt with. He needed to leave.

DG chugged his wine. "I've got to go. Just remembered I have to do something."

Maddy rose and accepted his empty glass. "It's still raining so be careful."

"Thanks for the wine. I probably won't see you until Monday as I have a new job tomorrow morning and won't be over until after lunch."

"I'm sure I'll be gone by then." She walked to the front door and opened it. "Have a good weekend. I'll see you Monday."

He walked past her and his arm lightly brushed against her breast. Damn, he was acting like an idiot. He turned back to her, standing on the porch. "I forgot to mention to you that the tile for the hall bath is on back order. We'll do it last but it might create a timing problem." That was better; keep all their conversations about the job.

"Should I pick out something else? I can't change the date of my party."

"Let's see how it goes. I'll have a better idea by the middle of next week."

"Okay, please let me know."

"Will do, see you later." He turned and hurried to his truck, splashing through a puddle at the end of the walk. He quickly backed out of the driveway and turned for home. The wipers beat a steady rhythm as he drove. Maybe they'd beat some sense into his head concerning Maddy.

He might be attracted to her but that was all. Long term relationships weren't his thing. And he was too old to change his ways. Right? Absolutely right. He wouldn't think about her. Surely that would solve his problem of falling for her.

Week Two: Thursday

Maddy loved San Antonio. She loved the history, the food, and the Paseo del Rio, or Riverwalk. Sure, it was a tourist mecca but she didn't care. It had shopping, great food, and beautiful walking trails. She'd visited many times and never tired of the city.

She arrived mid-afternoon and changed into cool clothing and a pair of walking sandals. Then she spent two hours wandering through La Villita Arts Village visiting boutiques and art galleries. The buildings dated back to the mid-1800s and were made of caliche clay blocks and stucco. Carrying a small oil painting for her entry way, a set of red chili tea towels, and goat milk hand soap, she walked down through the stone benches of the Ameson River Theater to the river.

She dined on chicken enchiladas in green sauce and an excellent margarita while watching people walk along the river. She'd waved at little kids in the famous riverboats providing tours of the Riverwalk. After a bit of television she called it a night. The seminar the next day on the calculation of bond rebate arbitrage would be boring but necessary for her CPA practice. A good night's sleep would help her to stay awake through it.

Week Two: Friday

The morning dawned sunny and warm. The local weather man said it was already seventy-seven degrees and it wasn't quite nine o'clock. Maddy hurried across the lobby of the hotel heading for the escalator to the meetings rooms. She looked forward to coffee and a roll before the seminar. She noticed a piece of sculpture on a pedestal to her right and didn't notice a man looking at a cell phone who stood a few feet from the escalator. She slammed into a human wall.

Staggering backward, a strong pair of arms kept her from falling. "Maddy, are you okay? I'm sorry I wasn't paying attention."

She stepped backward and replaced her purse over her shoulder. What in the world was DG doing in San Antonio? "I'm fine. Why are you here?"

"Crisis trip."

"What?"

"One of my buddies from college is the manager here. He's having some major work done on his house and asked me to look over the plans."

"I see. Who's locking my house then?" He looked fantastic in khakis and a green golf shirt.

"My best foreman has the key. Don't worry, your house will be safe."

"All right, I trust you." She noticed a clock on the wall behind him and hated being late. "Look, I've gotta go." She stepped away toward the escalator.

"Wait. Are you staying here tonight?"

She nodded. "I'm driving back tomorrow."

"Have dinner with me then."

What? She was usually pooped after these seminars and had planned on getting room service. "Let's see how it goes. I'll have a drink with you."

"Great. Meet me in the hotel bar at six."

"Fine, have a good day." She reached the escalator and stepped on. She could feel DG's eyes on her as she ascended. She managed not to turn around and quickly stepped off in search of the meeting room.

The seminar lasted seven hours with too many details. The only true break was an hour off for a catered lunch, Mexican food, of course. She learned what she needed to know for a municipal client, making the trip worthwhile. Plopping on the hotel bed shortly after five, she had her first thought of DG since seeing him that morning.

What a coincidence they were staying at the same hotel. Or, maybe it wasn't a coincidence, maybe it was destiny. "Ha-ha." She chuckled at her own joke. The seminar had fried her brain. Thankfully, she had a few minutes to relax before meeting him in the bar.

Destiny or not, it was weird running into him in San Antonio. She hadn't told him what hotel she'd be staying at or what city for that matter. Yep, it's a fluke or a stroke of luck. It didn't matter. It would be fun to have a drink with a nice man after such a boring day.

After a quick shower and debating on wearing a jeans outfit or a flowered turquoise and white summer dress, she walked into the hotel bar. DG was easy to spot sitting at a low table in a corner. He stood when he saw her and walked to meet her.

"You look very pretty in that dress." His eyes skimmed her from top to bottom, with a hint of a smile and something in his eyes she couldn't quite identify.

"Thank you." Her cheeks warmed with pleasure at the way he looked at her.

"Would you like to sit at the bar or at a table?"

"The bar, I might fall asleep in one of those comfy looking chairs."

"The bar it is." With his hand against her back, he led her to the far end of the long oak bar. He pulled a stool out and waited for her to get seated. He flagged the bartender. "What do you want to drink? Wine?"

"No, I'll have a vodka tonic." Maddy had been warm all day long and a drink full of ice sounded perfect. She studied DG's profile as he talked to the bartender. He had such a strong nose and nice lips . . . kissable lips. Oops, where did that come from?

He turned his body around to face her, his forearm resting along the edge of the bar. "How was your seminar?"

"Long. It was good. I learned what I needed to help a client."

"Do you go to a lot of training?"

"Licensed CPA's are required to have a certain number hours of continuing education each year. I try to incorporate all the training I need for those hours. Once in a while I do a class or workshop that's specific to one client."

"Sounds like you work hard for your clients," he said with a leisurely smile

"I do my best. But surely you're the same. Don't you do all you can for your clients?"

His smile turned into a chuckle. "Yes, ma'am, I do. That's another thing we have in common."

The bartender interrupted their conversation by making a production of laying napkins on the bar followed by her cocktail and DG's beer. Maddy put her hand over her mouth to hide the giggle close to erupting. She'd never before seen so much drama over a napkin.

"Guess we got our drinks in style," DG said. "Now that we're free from work, tell me about yourself. What do you do for fun?"

"Fun?" she squeaked. She couldn't remember the last time she'd done anything just for the hell of it. Her life was devoted to the twins, her practice, and her friendship with Jules. She hardly saw her parents anymore since they'd retired to Florida and ran with the tennis crowd. "I'll be honest with you. I don't do much that's fun." She put her chin in her hand with her elbow resting on the bar. "I think I'm boring."

He immediately squeezed her forearm. "Nah, you're intense and dedicated. You take your responsibilities seriously."

She cocked her head. "I'm boring and responsible?"

"No. What I meant to say is you work too hard."

"You're right, I do." How many times had Roger told her that?—a hundred, a million? "I should find a hobby. Do something that's relaxing.

"Good idea. I golf for relaxation, swimming, too." He tapped the neck of his beer bottle against her glass. "You should try it."

"My ex-husband golfed, no thanks." She sipped her drink, her mind going over various activities to do for fun—photography, cooking, painting, writing, needlework, baking, European travel, gardening—lots of things. "I've always enjoyed taking pictures, and there's cooking and baking, too."

"Maybe you could combine them."

"Like how?"

"Take a picture of what you cook and bake?" His eyes crinkled with good humor.

She touched his arm in delight. "You may have something there. I could do a cookbook for my family. Doesn't that sound like fun?"

His eyes darted from side to side. "I don't know, does it?"

She punched him playfully on the arm. "Stop it. Writing a family cookbook would be a lot of fun for me."

'I think so, too." He leaned over and quickly kissed her forehead then finished his beer. "You hungry? I'm starving."

She hoped she wasn't blushing. He'd kissed her like it happened every day. It wasn't a big deal, but . . . wow. "I do need to eat dinner."

He rose from the stool and stood behind it, tossing a couple of bills on the bar. "Come on then. We can find a restaurant on the Riverwalk."

Why not? Eating with a handsome man was better than room service any day. She slipped off the stool and walked with him to the hotel's elevator leading to the river.

DG grabbed Maddy's hand as soon as they reached the walk along the river. It was crowded and he didn't want to get separated from her. They turned to the right. "What would you like to eat? Mexican, Italian, a burger?"

"I had Mexican last night. How about Italian?" Maddy glanced at him and smiled—her mouth so sweet and kissable.

"Italian it is. There's a restaurant across this next bridge."

They walked in silence, with DG enjoying the sights and sounds from the river. He appreciated the years and years of hard work that had resulted in the Riverwalk. It was actually a huge park that boasted colorful gardens, twinkly lights, and seasonal decorations. Of course, in late June it was hot.

They soon came to a restaurant that DG knew and stopped to look at the menu posted along the walk.

"This looks good," she commented, standing close to him. He could smell her perfume and refused to acknowledge the image of a naked Maddy it fashioned in his head.

DG nodded quickly and stepped to the reception desk. "Table for two."

"Yes sir, we have open tables inside but nothing on the patio."

That worked for DG. He needed air conditioning. "Maddy, inside okay?"

"Yes, please, it's hot out here."

One more thing they had in common. The list was endless which gave him fewer and fewer excuses not to fall for her. He put a hand on her back as she followed the young girl up a short flight of steps to the inside. They were seated along a wall of windows that looked out to the patio. He liked the location.

"This is nice," Maddy said, opening her menu. "It's like being on the patio but with air conditioning."

Damn, they thought alike, too. "Would you like wine since we're eating Italian?"

"Sounds good." Maddy studied the menu and didn't look at him. After a moment she closed it.

"You've decided already?" He hadn't opened his yet since he'd been too busy watching her.

"Yes, I'm a fast study with menus. What wine are you ordering?"

"Our favorite Texas wine."

"Mm, good." She looked toward the window.

He looked at the menu and decided on his usual Italian dish. He watched Maddy. God, she was beautiful, and smart. The dress she wore showed off her slender waist and a good dose of cleavage and he liked it. His jeans tightened in response. *Whoa boy, don't get ahead of yourself.*

The waiter arrived with water and breadsticks, a good distraction. He ordered the wine and settled back in the chair.

Maddy pushed a strand of hair behind her ear. He'd love to take her hair out of the ponytail and run his hands through it. It probably felt like silk, the way her skin felt. He wiggled in the chair. What the hell was wrong with him?

"You're awfully quiet," she said.

"Sorry, thinking about my friend's house plans." At least that's what he should've been thinking about. *Get it together, Goodwin. This isn't your first rodeo.*

Maddy couldn't believe she was doing what she was doing—taking the elevator to the hotel's fifth floor and its outdoor pool and hot tub. Thankfully she had her bathing suit with her as she'd planned to swim laps Saturday morning. Fortunate as well since DG had made a joke about skinny dipping.

They'd had a wonderful dinner and then decided to get in the hot tub once back at the hotel. Why not? As DG had said, she needed more fun in her life. She walked through double glass doors to the pool area. It was lit with twinkly lights in the trees and colored lights behind potted palms. She spotted DG on the far side of the pool and walked around empty lounge chairs.

"Where are the people," she said when she reached him.

"It's late." He pointed to the hot tub. "Ready to get in?"

"Absolutely." She shrugged off the hotel bathrobe on to a deck chair then slipped in the bubbling water. "This is hot." She sat on a low ledge that circled the tub.

"It'll get better." DG trudged in, sitting across from her and stretching his arms along the edge of the tub. "Won't take long before your muscles relax."

They sat in a comfortable silence for a couple of minutes. A waiter carrying a tray crossed the pool area and knelt by the hot tub.

"Mr. Goodwin, I have your order." DG signed the ticket then the waiter handed a champagne flute to Maddy and to DG. "Have a good night."

"This is a surprise," Maddy said, already feeling her limbs unwind in the water. "Champagne usually goes straight to my head. You've been warned."

"Thanks for the warning," he said while raising his glass for a toast. "Here's to the beginning of a new and long lasting friendship."

Hmmm, that was sweet. She tapped her flute against DG's and sipped the wine. "You know, you're a surprising man."

He scooted a bit closer to her on the bench. "How am I surprising?"

"The first time we talked you seemed very business-like and uh, straight-laced, sorta—"

"No fun?" His mouth twisted drolly as he spoke.

"No, I meant, uh . . . yeah, no fun." She wanted to submerge herself in the hot tub to get away from the look of amusement on his face.

He floated off the bench and knelt in the water facing her. "No fun, huh? That's my take on being a professional and convincing a potential client that I'm, meaning my company, is good at remodeling and building things." He leaned towards her, a wicked gleam in his eyes. "This is the fun part of me."

Maddy knew this would happen—two single adults, a hot tub, and champagne—as his arms circled her shoulders and pulled her towards him. His lips hovered over her mouth for the briefest of moments before he made contact, lips to lips.

His assault started easy, feathery kisses getting to know the territory. Maddy moved toward him and the pressure of his lips increased as her mouth opened. He took advantage and tasted her with the tip of his tongue. A flame lit low in her belly. She wrapped her arms around him and allowed him greater access. A moan escaped as he nibbled her jaw line then kissed the sensitive area below her earlobe. His hand stroked her side, barely brushing against her breast.

They scooted closer together with her legs circling his waist. He kissed her deeply, one hand entangled in her hair while the other rubbed her back. Maddy's heart threatened to beat out of her chest. She'd never been kissed like this and she didn't want it to ever stop. It could easily become an addiction.

She sucked in a breath and pulled back from him, the heat was too intense. "Stop, I need to catch my breath."

He looked at her with dazed eyes. "My god, I'm sorry. I don't know what got over me." He moved back from her and sat on the bench next to her.

"It's okay." She pushed her hair back from her face then looked at him. "It takes two so don't feel bad."

A young couple holding hands walked to the edge of the hot tub. "Do you mind if we join you?" the man said.

Maddy rose. "We were just leaving so enjoy." She stepped out and retrieved the robe, wrapping is tightly around her.

DG did the same and walked with her to the pool entrance. He held the door open for her. "What time are you leaving tomorrow?"

"Probably about ten. I always go to The Alamo before I leave."

"That's a tradition with you?"

"Uh-huh," she said as they waited for the elevator.

"Have breakfast with me."

"Aren't you tired of me?" She questioned whether it was a good idea to eat another meal with her contractor. Their kissing was a huge mistake and she didn't want to give him the wrong idea.

"No, of course not. We both have to eat, right?" The elevator door opened and he motioned for her to enter then punched the buttons for their floors.

"That's true." Oh, why not, she did have to eat. "I'll meet you in the coffee shop at eight." The elevator stopped and she waved at him as she stepped out.

"Good night, Maddy," he said as the doors closed.

She walked down the long hall to her room. What in the world was she doing hanging out on a personal basis, in a freaking hot tub no less, with her contractor? She shook her head. On the other hand, kissing a man in a hot tub wasn't against the law. They participated equally. Having a hunky contractor was simply a bonus for a remodeling project. She slid the card key in and opened her door, looking forward to Saturday morning.

Week Two: Saturday

The negative fairies visited Maddy overnight. She woke quickly, after a hotel door down the hall slammed and shook the wall. "People are so rude," she muttered and rolled over, eying the digital clock, 6:04 a.m.

"Crap, ugh," she moaned.

Rolling to her back, she picked up the TV remote, no way could she get back to sleep. She clicked on the local news for the weather and wasn't surprised—hot, sunny, and hot. After sighing dramatically, she swung her legs to the floor and sat on the edge of the bed. Might as well have a cup of coffee while she debated how to tell DG she wasn't meeting him for breakfast.

Last night she'd convinced herself it was okay, but in her heart she knew it wasn't. She had no business canoodling with her contractor. She shivered and put her hands over her face for a moment, attempting to block out the fact that she had kissed him in a romantic hot tub. Yes, she admitted, it had been romantic, like out of a movie or a romance novel.

But this was real life and kissing her contractor who she had hired and given money to, was way out of bounds for proper behavior. Rubbing her forehead, she chastised herself for allowing the situation to get the best of her. So what if he was smart, nice, and handsome and sexy. Didn't matter—DG was off limits to her on a personal basis.

Her focus had to be on completing the remodel, and only that. Perhaps after the remodel was over they could talk about dating, it was only another two weeks at the most. She'd like that, but today . . . she couldn't face him after the hot tub. She fanned her face with her hand, damn, DG was one romantic contractor.

She rose from the bed and padded to the desk/bar combo to start the coffee. It brewed in the little one-cup-maker while she threw open the curtains and looked out the window. She couldn't see The Alamo but knew it was right behind the Rivercenter Mall, next to the Menger Hotel. She could have brunch at the Menger, it was fantastic food. But no, she wasn't that hungry and it would contradict what she'd be telling DG. She'd stop at the McDonald's on the way to The Alamo for coffee and a biscuit.

After adding fake sugar and powdered creamer to the coffee cup, she plumped the pillows on the bed and settled against them. It was time to face her dilemma. What and how to tell DG she wouldn't be meeting him for breakfast. She had options as to how to tell him—call him, go to his room, or send a text message. Texting would be the easiest.

She wouldn't lie to him. Bend the truth perhaps but not a full-blown lie. She'd wait a while to text him to make sure he was up.

Forty-give minutes later, she pulled her cell phone off the charger and clicked on DG's name in the contact list.

ME: Need to take rain check on breakfast, c u on Monday.

DG: k, anything wrong?

ME: No, need to get home.

Five minutes later, he replied.

DG: Drive safe.

She threw the phone on the bed and slid under the covers, pulling them up to her chin. "Crap, he's gonna hate me."

After a good dose of feeling sorry for herself, Maddy threw off the covers and staggered to the bathroom for a quick shower.

Within forty-five minutes she had coffee and a sausage biscuit and walked to the plaza in front of The Alamo. She sat on a park bench to eat her breakfast and people watch—lots of families and couples, a few singles like her. It was a simple pastime and one she enjoyed when she had time to spare.

Her heart snarled as she noticed a man reading one of the historic plaques who could be DG's twin. Then he moved to another and his walk wasn't like DG's. Whew. Meeting him at The Alamo would be embarrassing. She settled back and finished her food. Her mood had lightened with the beautiful weather and the excitement of once again strolling through the grounds of a Texas treasure.

She rose, threw her trash in a receptacle, and crossed the plaza to the entrance to The Alamo grounds. She walked through the gate and smiled at the volunteer handing out brochures. She meandered through the grounds on her way to the gift shop. Every time she visited the monument, something new caught her attention. This time is was the curve of a branch on a huge live oak. She pulled out her camera for a picture and once again noticed the DG look-alike on the other side of the tree by the Wall of History.

She focused on the man through the camera lens and zoomed in. Dammit, it *was* DG. Darting behind the massive tree, she debated what to do. Thankfully, he started walking toward the church, away from her. She scooted to her left, keeping DG in sight, and ran to the back door of the gift shop. She opened the heavy door and hurried inside, breathing a sigh of relief.

And then it hit her—she was acting like a complete imbecile.

She pushed the thought aside and moseyed around the store, looking at this and that, killing time. She hoped DG was already headed back to Sugar Land. After circling the store twice, she headed toward the food section for peach salsa, prickly pear chutney, and green pepper jelly. The brands were delicious and she stocked up every time she visited San Antonio.

After paying for her goodies, she went out the door facing the church and kept an eye out for a tall Texan. Things looked good so she rushed past the Menger and down Alamo Street. Now all she had to do was get in and out of the hotel without being noticed.

What? Her pace slowed, her heart flipped, dammit. She continued to act like a silly school girl. God love a duck. She'd embarrassed herself by avoiding a decent man who only wanted breakfast. So what if he was romance on a stick.

After claiming her overnight bag from the bell stand, Maddy waited outside the hotel for the valet to retrieve her car. Her mind was blank, she'd think about her behavior later, much later, maybe after Christmas. One of her most un-favorite things to do was acting stupid. And since she'd met DG, she'd made a career of it.

Week Three: Monday

Monday morning always started DG's week and meant several things to him—a fresh start on his jobs, a whole week with Trevor at home, a happy hour with Chad, and Sunday dinner with his parents. This Monday was the start of the third week on Maddy's job. Due to his bonehead moves in San Antonio, it had become exponentially more difficult.

He chewed on a red coffee stirrer as he drove to her house. He had to give his guys instructions for the day. She'd be there and he'd have to talk with her. Of course he'd talk with her, she was his client. He ran his fingers quickly through his hair, dumbfounded at his own foolishness.

He didn't know how to act so he'd pretend as if nothing had happened, like he hadn't kissed her, like he didn't think of her as more than a client. That would work. Pulling into her driveway, he stuck the stirrer in an empty cup and picked up his cell phone. Time to get this day on a roll as he had two other stops before a meeting at ten.

The garage door was open so he entered the house through the back. He could hear his guys talking in the kitchen and went there first. The last coat of paint would be applied to the cabinets and kitchen walls today, the granite installed tomorrow, the plumber and appliances installed on Wednesday.

Maddy would have Thursday and Friday to get everything stowed in the cabinets and drawers and prepare for her party. He'd added a couple of extra guys to make sure that would happen.

He'd also changed the timing for a part of the outside remodel, sprucing up the patio, to this week rather than next. The hot tub and new fence would have to wait until week four. Surely the speeded up construction schedule would make her happy.

"Hey boss, have a good trip to San Antonio?" Lucio, the head painter and a friend, asked as he mixed paint thinner into the cabinet enamel.

"It was okay." DG ran a hand over the side of a cabinet—smooth as silk, no brush marks.

"Did you see your lady friend?"

DG nodded, "Yeah, at lunch."

Lucio made a kissing sound. "Any after lunch action?"

"I'll never tell." Lucio assumed every woman DG knew was a conquest since women flocked to Lucio like fleas, despite the wedding ring he wore religiously. "We're on a tight schedule for the rest of the week. Today, finish painting the kitchen walls and cabinets, and make sure all of the baseboards are painted and caulked. Okay?"

"You got it." Lucio said, grinning and climbing a ladder to reach the top cabinet.

"Good, I'll see you later." DG retraced his steps through the garage and to his truck. One part of him had hoped to see Maddy while the other was glad he didn't have to face her. How sad was that? Real sad so he'd make sure he talked to her when he returned later in the day.

Maddy stepped out of the hallway, nodded at Lucio. DG hadn't realized she'd come out of her bedroom shortly after he'd arrived. She'd stopped when the painter asked him about his trip to San Antonio. Now she knew the truth—he went there to see a woman, not to look at house plans.

He lied to her.

She fisted her hands at her sides, anger coursing through every molecule in her body. Damn him. Damn him for lying to her. Damn him for kissing her and making her believe there could be a happily ever after despite a failed marriage and a crappy divorce.

Turning around, she went back to her bedroom to get her purse and keys. She needed to get out of the house and clear her head.

"I'll be gone for a couple of hours." She nodded curtly at Lucio and headed to her vehicle.

Once on the road she knew where to go to make her feel better. She stopped at a drive-thru for coffee, juice, and an egg-cheese biscuit and soon pulled into a parking lot and looked at the sign—Sugar Creek Dog Park. She loved to watch the dogs play with each other. It never failed to brighten her mood.

She chose a shaded bench with a good view of the large dog section of the park. She ate her breakfast while watching the dogs run and play with each other.

A few owners threw a ball or a Frisbee with the dogs retrieving, their tails wagging furiously. It was fun to watch such pure joy.

Then she thought of DG and scowled.

Thank heavens the remodeling was half over. Her interactions with him would be limited if she worked at it. He knew all the projects so they didn't need to discuss every little detail of the construction. She would make it work.

She tossed the paper bag from her breakfast in a trash can and started to walk around the perimeter of the park. The exercise would be good for her as it was a large park.

Walking was therapeutic. It usually allowed her mind to relax and roam from one subject to another. Unfortunately on this Monday morning, her thoughts continued to focus on DG.

Why did he have to be such a jerk?

Over the weekend she'd re-played their evening in San Antonio over and over in her head. There was nothing he'd said or done that had hinted at a girlfriend. In fact she'd decided it was silly to ignore her attraction. There was nothing stopping her other than her own foolishness. But she now wondered why he might be attracted to her.

She stopped at a drinking fountain and watched the dogs play. At least someone was having a good time.

"Urgghhh." She pushed thoughts of DG out of her head and quickened her pace. She'd circle the park another two times to work off the breakfast biscuit. Damn that man for getting her upset. She always overloaded on carbs and fat when something set her off.

Once she returned home, Maddy filled a bottle with ice water and retreated to her bedroom. She had another romance novel to read and a nap wouldn't hurt either. She was exhausted.

The progress on the remodel was much faster than she'd anticipated. No doubt DG had hurried up the work to get it completed ahead of schedule so he wouldn't have to deal with her. The bonus was that the party would proceed as scheduled. She was grateful for that.

Voices in the hallway woke Maddy. She had dozed off with the paperback on her chest. Someone knocked on the bedroom door. She rose and opened it.

"Sorry to bother you," DG said, a small smile crossing his lips. "We need to check the baseboards in here."

"Fine, of course, I'll get out of your way." She stepped aside for DG and Lucio to enter then went to the patio. The sky was once again covered in dark clouds which fit her mood perfectly. She sat in a chair and waited. She'd give it thirty minutes for DG to be done and leave. She only had to wait five.

"Maddy, we need to talk." DG stood in front of her, tall and resolute.

"Is there a problem with the kitchen?"

"No, but we need to talk." He sat on the edge of the chaise lounge.

"About what?"

"About San Antonio."

"Really?" She raised her chin and did her best to glower at him. "What about San Antonio?"

"You're not going to make this easy are you?"

She shrugged. "No clue what you're talking about." She pointed to the sky as the wind picked up. "Hurry up though, it's about to start raining."

"Why didn't you want to meet me for breakfast on Saturday morning?"

"Seriously, that's your question?" She couldn't believe his audacity. "I'm sure you ate with your girlfriend so what's the difference."

"Girlfriend?"

"Yeah, the one you had lunch with." She rose and leaned toward him, poking a finger in his chest. "Kissing me in the hot tub was a really rotten thing to do." She walked to the door and turned back to him as drops of rain spotted his shirt. "Let's make sure this remodel is completed as soon as possible."

In the kitchen Maddy heard the workers in the garage. They'd be leaving soon. Good, she needed alone time in her own house.

DG walked past her, his face a mask. "I'll see you in the morning, Mrs. Summers."

"I expect you will." She swore under her breath, the man had cojones. Why did she still find him so very attractive? Obviously, her brain and her heart needed to get on the same page.

DG once again drove in a downpour leaving Maddy's house. He had no clue what in the hell she'd been talking about—eating lunch with a girlfriend. He didn't have a girlfriend, in San Antonio or anywhere else. Where in the hell had she gotten that idea? He shook his head in disbelief. Understanding women was too damned hard.

He strummed his finger tips on the steering wheel. Why were they always throwing in complications to a relationship? Complications that served no purpose other than screwing up things that were going just fine. Maybe saying he had a girlfriend was her way of stopping anything going further between them.

His fist hit the steering wheel. Dammit, why didn't she just tell him to cool it rather than go through all these theatrics? He really liked Maddy but drama wasn't his style. Maybe he should boycott female clients altogether. That would probably make his life easier.

Week Three: Tuesday

Four days until the anniversary party. It was going to happen. The granite installation was today along with plenty of dust and noise. Shopping would get Maddy out of the house and away from the commotion, definitely a better alternative to hiding out in her bedroom with earplugs.

She entered her favorite home goods store for new bathroom towels and rugs, and anything else she might happen to find. With the new kitchen wall color she'd added turquoise as an accent and hoped to find a couple of cute accessories.

The turquoise gods were out in full force as she found a tall decorative bottle, a lamp for the foyer, a round placemat, and a candle holder. She also found a new yellow throw for her bed. Shopping wasn't on the top-ten list of things she enjoyed but the effort of scrutinizing the shelves was worth her time. She was pleased with her purchases.

After stopping at a crafts store for silk flowers and greenery she drove to Café Croissant to meet Jules for lunch. The little bistro was in a 1910 house in old Sugar Land. They loved it for the salads and the croissants of course.

Jules had arrived first and snagged a table next to a window overlooking the garden.

"Hey, missy." Maddy hung her purse on her chair and sat across from her friend. "Oh, it's good to be out of the house."

"Constant noise, dust, and workers getting to you?"

"I'm going nuts. Today is granite installation so you know that's noisy and dusty."

"I remember," Jules said as she picked up the wine list. "We have all afternoon to waste so let's get wine."

Maddy smiled at her dear friend who always knew what was what. "Count me in. I need the mental break."

"Break from what?"

"Let's talk after we eat." Maddy would put off talking about DG as long as she could. She wanted Jules's advice but had a hunch she'd feel like a fool once Jules had the full picture and expressed an opinion. Like that hadn't happened before.

Jules pressed her lips together for a moment. "Sounds good." She studied the wine list. "Red or white?"

"You decide, my brain is mush."

"Poor Maddy," Jules said, stifling a giggle. "You are so dramatic."

"Dramatic, my ass, I want a good cabernet."

Jules winked at her, "And so predictable."

Regardless of drama or predictability on Maddy's part, the food was fantastic. She loved their grilled shrimp Caesar salad and had managed to mimic the dressing after multiple attempts.

Jules dug into her Cobb salad with gusto. She finished it easily, using "It's super healthy and includes all the food groups," as her excuse.

Once the dishes were cleared, Jules got to the point. "What has turned your brain to mush and how was the trip to San Antonio?"

Maddy sat back in her chair with a sigh, dreading the conversation already. "Actually they're related."

"Really? This has got to be a great story."

"Very funny." Maddy sipped her wine, pondering where to start. "I don't think I actually told you that I'm attracted to my contractor but that's over now."

"Why? What happened?"

"We met up by *chance* in San Antonio, and had a very pleasant dinner together." She took a deep breath, forcing herself to continue. "Somehow, we ended up in the hot tub, and after one glass of champagne . . . well, one thing led to another and he kissed me and—"

Jules nearly jumped out of her chair. "He kissed you in a hot tub? This sounds promising . . . and hot."

"It *was* hot, a little too hot." She fanned herself, remembering the way she'd felt in his arms. "Things were moving a little too quickly so I stopped it." She placed her hands on the table and nodded. "As it turns out, it was the right thing to do."

"Tell me everything." Jules motioned to the waiter for another glass of wine.

Maddy gave her a summary version of the hot tub scene and full details of all else through yesterday evening. "Over the weekend I realized it was silly not to go to breakfast with him. What's wrong with us seeing each other? There's only a few more days on the remodel." She sighed. "I thought he was such a good guy and then I find out he has a girlfriend."

Jules scrunched her face. "Why do you think he has a girlfriend?"

"Were you not listening to me? I told you he had lunch with a woman in San Antonio."

"I think it's possible you've made an incorrect assumption based on smack-talk from a couple of guys."

Maddy sent her traitorous friend an irritated glare.

"One simple conversation could clear this up, one way or the other." Jules patted Maddy's hand resting on the table. "Tell him what you heard. Maybe there's a good explanation for it. If not, you did the right thing."

Maddy felt the blood drain from her face. Leave it to Jules to shed some light on both sides of the mystery. "You really think this could all be a huge misunderstanding?"

"It's possible. Talk to him about it. If it is, tell him you made a mistake. If he's a good guy, he'll understand."

Maddy found herself considering Jules' suggestion. "Maybe you're right."

Jules, a lover of the last word in any situation, leaned forward and gave her a pat on the hand. "If I am, don't forget to beg for forgiveness."

Week Three: Wednesday

The granite looked spectacular. Maddy had selected the same pattern for the kitchen and both bathrooms. She congratulated herself on her good taste and decorative knowhow as she plugged in her coffee pot for a much needed jolt of caffeine before DG and his crew arrived.

Today was appliance day. By the end of it, she'd have a six-burner gas stove in her kitchen, along with a built-in wine cooler, new dishwasher, double ovens, and microwave. But the stove was the main attraction. She'd chosen the same type of gas range she'd had in the home she shared with Roger. The stove-top and the oven were the perfect match of technology and pizazz. She could only hope the new one worked as well as her old one had.

A plumber arrived on her doorstep mid-morning to set the new gas line for the range. She waited all morning for some sign of DG, to no avail. Of course, the one morning she really wanted to talk with him.

By three o'clock all appliances were installed and ready to go. Spinning around in her kitchen, she could at least applaud these particular choices. Everything looked wonderful and she couldn't wait to start cooking. She turned at the sound of a footstep; her heart immediately began pounding overtime.

Her hand went to her chest. "DG, geez, you scared me."

"Sorry, we get used to coming in without knocking."

"That's okay." Maddy calmed herself quickly then watched him. Would he be willing to talk with her? "Don't you think the appliances look great?"

He walked around her, keeping his distance, to inspect the latest additions to her kitchen. "Looks good. Are you happy with your selections?"

"Very much so." One step toward him, and he moved to the other side of the island.

"Glad to hear that. Tomorrow we'll finish the hall bath and stain the patio."

"I thought that would be next week."

"Moved it up so your patio will look nice for your party."

"Thank you for thinking of that." This was Maddy's opening to talk with him. "I'm glad you're here, I need to talk with you."

He seemed to bristle at that. "Talk about what?"

"Actually . . . I may need to apologize to you, if I jumped to a wrong conclusion about you having a girlfriend. Especially since I didn't give you a chance to explain." She wasn't sure how her words were settling with him as his face was blank. "A friend of mine made me realize the quickest way to clear the air is to talk about it."

"Maddy, I don't know where you got that idea. I don't have a girlfriend. I think I told you that a couple of weeks ago when we talked about your party."

She bit her lower lip, unsure of how to tell him she'd eavesdropped on his and Lucio's conversation. "I'm not accustomed to anyone calling me a liar. We'll be out of your hair soon." He turned and headed for the garage.

Maddy scooted around the island. "Wait. What time will you be here tomorrow?"

He spoke without turning around. "I'm not sure," he said, before letting himself out the back door.

"Crap, that didn't go as planned at all." Maddy shrugged. She was tired of dealing with strangers in her home and the emotional ups and downs of thinking about DG. She'd messed up their one chance for any kind of a relationship. It was over, finished before it really started. She didn't have the courage to try talking with him again. This rejection rang all too loudly in her mind.

Week Three: Thursday

DG met Chad for an early breakfast at the Smokehouse Diner on Highway 6. It was a longstanding Thursday morning tradition, a chance to catch up with each other, and discuss their families, and talk without a filter.

Chad sat in his usual spot at the counter. DG waved to Lily, their waitress for the last ten years. She had a cup of coffee on the counter before he sat on the stool.

"Thanks, Lily." He turned to Chad. "How you doing, cuz?"

"Just fine, cuz. What's got a bur up your butt?"

"Why do you think that?" DG had wondered more than once if his cousin had psychic capabilities. He could read moods like no one else.

"Just a hunch." Chad held a coffee cup to his lips and eyed DG over the top. "Wanna tell me about it?"

"Jesus, you're spooky."

Lily approached, holding her order pad and sporting a sly grin. "Okay gents, what can I get you today?"

"The usual," DG and Chad said at the same time.

Lilly clapped her hands. "I'm clairvoyant. I knew that's what you'd order."

Chad chuckled at the waitress. "No great feat, seeing as how predictable we are." He jabbed an elbow in DG's side. "Tell me what's got you dancing like a defrocked rooster."

DG rolled his eyes. "You want to know the truth? I'll tell you the truth—it's a damned client. She's got me going in circles."

Chad perked up at that comment. "Circles, huh?"

"Yeah, things were going great in the hot tub when I kissed her and then boom, she accuses me of having a girlfriend. I can't deal with a woman like that."

Chad blinked and blinked again. "You kissed a client . . . in a hot tub? What the hell is wrong with you?"

DG opened his mouth to respond then closed it. This situation was complicated. "In another week she won't be a client."

"She must be a special lady. Go for it." Apparently Chad did have psychic skills.

"We had some kind of misunderstanding, apparently. I'm still in the dark about that."

"I still say go for it. If a chick has you in this much of a tailspin, there must me some chemistry. Talk to her, do what you can to clear it up." Chad raised an index finger. "It's better to regret something you do than something you don't do."

"When did you become so philosophical?"

"Since the wife has me eating fiber."

This had been a good day. Maddy managed to add a plastic liner to the new cabinet shelves and drawers, and empty a ton of boxes. The new kitchen turned out better than she'd imagined. DG's team had done an excellent job building the cabinetry and installing the granite and backsplash.

Tomorrow she'd clean, again, and go to the grocery store. Her to-buy list for the party increased in length by the hour. She had DG to thank for getting the remodel done in time for the one year anniversary of her divorce. It might seem a silly celebration to others but to Maddy, it was her own personal declaration of independence.

She'd married so young, right out of college, and had never had the opportunity to live alone, until her separation and subsequent divorce. Having a house to oneself was an exhilarating experience.

DG's team had been going over things in the house but worked mostly in the backyard. They'd finished staining the patio concrete, and completed a railing around the edge. She could see the outline of a flagstone walk leading to the new gazebo and hot tub. By the end of next week, the entire project would be completed and she'd no longer see DG on a daily basis.

Yeah. That kind of sucked.

He'd made his feelings clear yesterday. He wanted nothing to do with her and her tendency to over-dramatize any situation. She'd blown it and that was that. Her insecurities about men, dating, and life in general, had caused her to act like a jealous shrew. Accusing a man she barely knew of having a girlfriend, without solid evidence, was simply too much.

Jules would tell her to talk with him one last time. What could it hurt other than her pride? At this point pride was irrelevant. She'd regret it if she didn't at least make the attempt. She glanced at the clock on the microwave. Where was he? The workers had already left for the day and he always checked on their work.

He probably couldn't stand to be around her. *Great.*

Pushing past her feelings of dejection, she loaded the last drawer then retrieved a wine bottle themed print and a couple of ceramic wall plaques off the dining room table. Her favorite was a ribbon decorated with grapes and the saying "Live Well, Love Much, Laugh Often." She went to the garage for a ladder and a hammer.

She set the ladder at the right spot in the kitchen. The doorbell rang as she placed her foot on the first step. She debated about going to the door. No one ever visited her. The bell rang again so she stepped down and went to answer it.

DG stood on her porch, his hands behind his back. Her heart pounded at the sight of him, standing there in just tight enough jeans and a crisp, white T-shirt.

"I figured you weren't coming by today."

"Behind schedule." He smiled and reached out to her with a bouquet of yellow roses.

Maddy's mouth formed an "O" as she accepted the flowers from him. "Thank you. Do you give flowers to all your clients?"

"I'm giving them to my friend, not my client."

She smiled and stepped aside, not exactly sure of what to make of the situation, but hoping for the best. "Come on in."

He followed her to the kitchen, remained silent as she arranged the flowers in a crystal vase.

She set the vase on her new gold and brown granite counter. "They made good progress in the back today."

"I'll go check." He went out the patio door.

While he was outside she ran to her bathroom to check her hair and face. Gawd, she looked like a zombie. She brushed her hair and pulled it back in a low ponytail then pinched her cheeks and brushed on lip gloss. Anything more and it'd look like she'd been primping, which she had, but it didn't need to be obvious.

DG reentered the kitchen through the back door.

"Is everything okay?" She walked around the island, keeping it between them as a buffer.

"Yes, we'll put the furniture back tomorrow and pour the cement base for the hot tub. Sorry we couldn't get it done in time for your party."

"That's not a problem. The hot tub is for me."

"You won't invite a friend to enjoy it with you?"

DG's behavior confused her—bringing her flowers and talking about the hot tub with a twinkle in his eye. "I hadn't thought that far ahead. Right now I'm focused on cleaning and grocery shopping for the party."

"I hope I'm still invited."

"Well, sure . . . but I assumed you wouldn't be interested."

"Why?"

"Yesterday you said you didn't deal with drama . . . and, well, I was acting a bit dramatic, accusing you of having a girlfriend."

"Where did you get that idea?"

"I overheard you telling Lucio you had lunch with a woman in San Antonio and it sounded like he was asking you about a girlfriend."

He ran his fingers through his hair, mussing it to the point of let-me-run-my-hands-through-it-sexy-as-hell. "I did have lunch with a woman, Julie, we've been friends since grade school. She's Jim's wife, the buddy I told you about. I looked at their house plans."

"Oh."

"Lucio always talks like that when it comes to women. He's in denial that he's happily married and the father of triplets."

"Oh." Maddy felt heat rush from her toes to the end of every strand of hair. "I feel really silly. I jumped to a conclusion and . . . I'm so sorry."

"I'm sorry, too. I should've told you about Julie yesterday." He took a cautious step around the island. "Is it okay if I hug you?"

She nodded, closing her eyes as his arms wrapped around her. He smelled so good. He felt so good. She pulled back from him. "Thank you for giving me a second chance."

"You're worth a little drama." He kissed her then ran a finger along her jawline. "Hey, I brought something. I'll be right back." He hurried to the foyer and out the front door.

He returned carrying a cooler and set it on the island counter.

"What's this?" Maddy said, curiosity strumming along her spine.

"I thought I'd provide happy hour this time." He looked at her, hope in his eyes. "That is, assuming you're happy to have me here."

"I'm very happy you're here."

"Good." He opened the cooler and pulled out a bottle. "I thought we might try another brand of red I like." He had a wide, open smile as he showed her the label.

"Estancia, love it!" She cocked her head and squinted at him. "How did you know this is one of my favorite wines?"

"I didn't." He bent over and kissed her lips. "But we do have the same taste in wine. Where's a corkscrew?"

She handed him the bottle opener and opened a couple of cabinets before finding glasses. "I need to remember where I've put things."

"I brought snacks, too." DG went back to the cooler. He brought out two plastic containers, a box of wheat crackers, and potato chips. "I made a salmon spread and onion dip. Two appetizers I know how to make."

"I'm impressed."

"Don't be until you try them. I provide snacks for poker night. Anything tastes good with beer."

Maddy laughed, it felt so good to be back to normal with DG. Although she wasn't sure what "normal" meant for them, she'd take it. She dipped a cracker into the salmon spread and popped it into her mouth. *Delicious.*

They organized their impromptu happy hour on the island counter. DG carried the stools from the garage while Maddy poured the wine.

Once they were both seated, he raised his glass. "I'd like to make a toast if that's okay."

"Of course." Maddy nodded and held her glass close to DG's.

He cleared his throat then began. "Here's to friendship and to more if you're willing to go on a journey with me."

"A journey?"

"I'd like to think that you and I are dating . . . going steady, maybe."

"Hmm . . . dating you . . . okay. Going steady, nah, I think we're a tad too old." She winked at him.

"Ah, we're more the dating with benefits crowd." He rubbed his hand along the top of her thigh.

"That's what I'm thinkin'" She tapped her glass against his then tasted the wine. "Mm, so good."

DG hadn't realized it before, but he'd been holding his emotions in check, waiting to see Maddy's reaction to him, especially after he'd been such a jerk yesterday. But her killer reaction to his toast gave him a definite sense of hope. Hope that he had met the woman who would someday change his single ways.

"Do you need help with anything for the party?"

"Sure, I could use help with the ice. I'll need several bags for the beer and soft drinks."

"I can do that. Anything else?" He was pleased she didn't question him attending the party.

She gave him one of her cute giggles. "I like your salmon spread. Would it be too much trouble to bring that, along with the recipe?"

That was the last thing he expected her to say. He rose, stepped to her. He cupped her face with his hands and smiled. "I'd be honored." He kissed her, sweetness comingled with need.

"Good," she murmured against his lips.

He kissed her again and this kiss was anything but gentle. His hands stroked her back and settled on her waist. Passion, heated and quick, flared between them, like a fire catching at a stick of kindling. He pulled back from her and pressed his forehead against hers. "You turn me on."

Maddy lifted her arms and wound them around DG pulling him against her. "Ditto. You feel so good."

He kissed the top of her head. "Baby, you have no idea how good you feel."

She chuckled in that way women do when they know they're totally in control of the situation. He didn't give a damn what she controlled. His was so lucky he'd met her.

He wanted to make love with her but understood the timing wasn't right. She deserved to be romanced and he wanted their first time to be perfect and special. He'd figure out something to let her know how crazy he was about her. Did he already love this woman? He pulled back enough to stare down at her beautiful face. Good chance.

Week Three: Saturday — The Anniversary Party

Maddy had accomplished much of the party preparation on Friday so Saturday was devoted to last minute cleaning and setting out the food and drinks. DG arrived late afternoon with ice and his salmon spread.

"Thanks for helping me," Maddy said as she kissed his cheek.

"No problem. Where do you want the ice?" He carried five bags in his arms.

She led him to the kitchen and a huge cooler on the floor filled with beer, soft drinks, and water. "I'll take one bag and add it to the wine." She'd set up a round galvanized bucket to hold various wine bottles so her guests could help themselves.

Within minutes the preparations were completed and the doorbell rang. Maddy went to the answer it and welcomed Jules and her hubby, Jeff, to the celebration.

"Hey guys, come on in and check out my new kitchen."

DG leaned against a counter, looking right at home. Maddy introduced everyone and the doorbell rang again.

DG glanced at her and nodded toward the door. "Go ahead. I'll get these guys set up with drinks."

An hour later the party was in full swing with over thirty people inside and outside Maddy's home. Everyone loved her master bath and the kitchen, of course. Her voice purred with pride as she explained that DG was the contractor who did the remodel. He graciously answered questions about plugged toilets and dripping faucets.

Jules pulled Maddy into the dining room. DG and Jeff were on the patio talking golf and making plans to play the next day.

Jules hugged Maddy. "I am so happy for you. Your house is beautiful and DG is perfect for you."

"How can you say that? We've known each other less than a month."

Maddy stood back and wagged an index finger back and forth. "Have you not listened to me at all when it comes to men and relationships?"

"Sure I have." Regardless, she needed to know DG longer than three weeks before she'd state they were perfect for each other. Although they did seem to have a compatibility that she had never shared with Roger. "Do you believe in soul mates?"

"You bet I do. I knew Jeff was meant for me the first time I heard him speak in English class, sophomore year. Granted we weren't married for another ten years. He needed to be mature enough to understand it was inevitable—but I always knew we were perfect for each other."

"Geez, in ten years I'll almost be eligible for the senior discount at Denny's."

"DG is already mature." Jules smiled easily and calmly. "I see the way he looks at you. Sweet pea, he is one hundred percent over the moon for you."

That comment warmed Maddy's heart. She was over the moon for DG as well. But being the practical CPA, she vowed she wouldn't get ahead of herself—one day at a time as her granny used to say.

Four hours later, Maddy relaxed with DG in side by side chairs on the patio. She was tired and pleased with her one-year-after-the-divorce celebration.

"I think the party was a success," she said. She turned her head toward DG. "You hit it off with Jeff."

"He seems like a good guy. We'll see how he swings tomorrow on the golf course."

"I believe he was on the golf team in college."

"He didn't mention that."

"I hope you didn't make any bets with him." Maddy grinned. She loved her friends and she loved that DG had met them and they'd all enjoyed each other. It was a new experience, since Roger had never liked Jules. Thank god that part of her life was over. This was a new day with DG.

"Nah, I'm not that stupid." He rolled his head against the back of the chair toward her. "Hey, I'm glad I met you."

She reached out to clasp his hand. "Me, too."

He grabbed it and brought it to his mouth, kissing the top. "Good. I figure we have years and years ahead of us."

Maddy's eyes welled with tears. She brushed them away but not before DG noticed.

"What's wrong?"

"Nothing, feeling sentimental."

"About what?"

"I'm not sure." She didn't know what to say. She felt weird, overwhelmed, out-of-sorts.

DG squeezed her hand. "Seems to me you've had some major changes lately."

"Oh, yeah?"

"Absolutely, your kids' departure for college, so soon after your divorce, purchasing a house on your own. You've spent hard-earned money on remodeling it. I'm sure there's something else. And then the frosting on the cake, you met me."

"All that is true." She sucked in a breath and let it out slowly, watching the palms sway in a light evening breeze. The last year had been stressful and emotional. She been pulled one way and then the other, and had finally made her way through it. Buying this house had meant so much to her. Remodeling it to her liking, especially the kitchen, had truly been a blessing. She was a lucky lady to have such good fortune.

"You know what?" she said, her heart thudding faster than normal. "I'm very glad I met you. I love frosting."

"Babe, you came to the right man. I have all kinds of sugar."

Maddy swung her legs over the side of her chair, leaning in to DG. "Lucky for you I have a sweet tooth."

He circled his arms around her and pulled her onto his lap. She giggled, stopping at the look on his face. Her hand brushed his cheek. "You look so serious."

"Not serious, just grateful I found my girl," he whispered. His arms tightened around Maddy as he placed his cheek against hers. "I know we need to go slow since we haven't known each other that long. You just tell me when the right amount of time has passed."

She sucked in a breath, this man had the sweetness of a saint. "I think we need to get the remodeling finished so I'm not a client."

"I agree," he said as he planted a kiss on her neck.

"How about we bat a homerun a week from tonight in my new hot tub?" The anticipation of DG, the hunk, in her own spa had Maddy imagining all sorts of activities.

"Count me in," he whispered, nibbling at her earlobe, and then her neck while his hands caressed her arms and back.

"Just don't forget . . ." Maddy's eyelids fluttered closed at the feel of his teeth nipping gently at her ear, her neck. Hope surged in her heart. Hope for happiness and a future filled with love. She said a quick prayer of thanks for this wonderful man coming into her life.

"Don't forget what, baby?" he whispered into her ear, causing chills to break out over her skin.

"The frosting," she whispered. "Lots and lots of frosting . . ."

MADDY'S ASPARAGUS ROLLS

Ingredients
3 loaves whole wheat or white sandwich bread
3 cans whole asparagus spears, or blanched fresh
6 sticks softened butter
3 oz parmesan cheese
2 T garlic salt or to taste

Instructions
Drain asparagus on a paper towel. Remove crusts from bread. Thoroughly mix cheese and garlic salt in butter. Spread butter mixture on each slice of bread with a pastry brush. Roll each slice around an asparagus spear, flatten slightly. Place all slices, seam side down, in a buttered baking dish. Spread remaining butter mixture on top of rolls. Bake at 350 degrees for 30 minutes, until top is golden brown. Cut each slice into thirds for smaller portions if desired. Makes 60 rolls, approximately.

Note: Freezes well before baking

DEDICATION

Maddy and DG's story is dedicated to all the wonderful general contractors who do residential remodeling. You bring much happiness to weary homeowners who have exhausted any talent they might have for DIY projects. A special thanks to Chad Howard, my own contractor who did a marvelous job with my remodel. I sure wish he installed hot tubs.

ABOUT THE AUTHOR

Karen Sue Burns

Karen has been a writer since 8th grade. Her day job as a CPA has provided interesting experiences: travel to Rio de Janeiro, London, and Oslo, auditing wine bottle glass molds in California, and taking a helicopter to a drillship off the Texas Gulf Coast. Accounting has been good to her, but writing romance and mystery novels is her passion. She enjoys cooking and creating recipes so her heroines do the same. All of her indie anthologies and novels include one of her favorite recipes. _In Hot Pursuit_ is her debut romantic suspense novel and _The Liberation of Mr. Delaney_ is her first indie published novel. She is also a contributor to the sweet and sensual romance anthology series _Seasons of Love_ with the books _Hearts, Hearths and Holidays; Spring Promise; Sweet Summertime Love; and Christmas by Candlelight._ Readers may contact Karen via the Bio/Contact tab on her website. Check out the Recipe tab while you're there!

Find Karen Here:

Website: http://karensueburns.com
Facebook: http://facebook.com/KarenSueBurns
Twitter: http://twitter.com/karensueburns
Blog: http://karensueburns.com/blog
Pinterest: http://pinterest.com/KarenSueBurns

ONCE UPON A SUMMER'S KISS
By
Carmine Valentine

To the residents of Bellingham, Washington, please excuse my imagination. For the purpose of this story, I have placed an island in the middle of Lake Whatcom. Adventure happens there. So does a little romance…

Chapter One

The sweet and hypnotic music of Etta James' *At Last* weaved its magic through the warm summer night. This song always brought Samantha Flowers to a point where she almost stopped breathing and literally stopped thinking practical thoughts. It simply wasn't fair.

How was she going to get through the wedding rehearsal party avoiding a man she'd only just met and couldn't stop thinking of when a song like that slipped into her bloodstream like the headiest of intoxicants? Even worse; at tomorrow's wedding, he'd be standing with the groom, and she with the bride.

To add to her dilemma, couples followed the prospective bride and groom to the terrace where a fairyland canopy of thousands of tiny lights softly lit the dance floor. Now, more than ever, she needed to avoid Cole's attention. A dance with him would surely weaken her resolve.

After a dance with the bride's uncle and a young nephew, she noticed that Cole made to move in her direction. Samantha slipped away between the dancers and found a secluded spot by the honeysuckle vine that climbed up the brick wall. The glow of candlelight from the tables, Tiki torches, and pots of large palm trees added a tropical atmosphere. The warm breeze caressed her bare shoulders in the halter-style gown she wore and teased a blond curl from the chignon at the nape of her neck.

She glanced over the railing at the boats in the marina below, bobbing gently on the waters of the quiet bay. Bellingham, Washington was the groom's hometown and the wedding would be held here tomorrow, as well. The groom and his cousin had graduated from the college in this town. The very cousin her friend Margo had introduced to Samantha, immediately upon her arrival this afternoon. She couldn't help but notice that Cole's gaze had strayed to her more than once over the course of the elegant salmon dinner.

Through the slow-moving dancers, Cole's lean build and broad shoulders were easy to spot across the terrace. Two of the bride's coworkers, wearing suggestive smiles on their pretty faces, conversed with him as they sipped on champagne and swayed their hips to the beat of the music. Samantha wondered how long it would take before Cole finally got the hint and asked one of them to dance. She looked back at him, found his gaze pinned on her as he sipped from a tumbler of amber liquid. The wink he sent her direction had her spinning on her heels.

Caught in the act. What the heck was she doing? Watching him when she should have been sending the opposite message by avoiding him at all costs. She fidgeted, suddenly self-conscious in her ice blue dress, with its daringly low-cut back. The silky material brushed her thighs as she stepped through the doors where guests mingled over desert or at the bar. She nearly plowed into Rita, the wedding planner.

"Oh, dear," Rita shook her short, red hair. "I believe we have a romance dodger in our midst."

"Pardon me?" Samantha replied.

"Don't think I haven't seen romantic sparks flying. The object is not to run in the opposite direction, my dear."

Without warning, Rita whisked a small, red-capped, perfume-sized bottle from her sequined purple apron. She sprayed the contents on the pulse points of Samantha's wrist, sending the scent of jasmine wafting through the air.

"That potion usually does the trick." Rita pocketed her bottle and cocked her head slightly, as if summoning some internal radar. "I believe I just heard someone's button pop off."

Margo had warned her about the wedding planner's quirky ways. She took some getting used to, but had a heart of gold, and meant well.

Two of Samantha's friends, also members of the wedding party, stood near the bar. Samantha joined them and used a cocktail napkin from the bar to wipe off the moisture on her arm.

"I see you've met Rita." Connie smiled, stunning in a red dress with spaghetti straps and a slit up to her thigh. She tucked her short blond hair behind her ears, setting a pair of large silver hooped earrings in motion. . "She clipped a string off the hem of my dress. What did she help you with?"

Samantha held up the inside of her wrist.

"Mm, you smell nice, almost too nice," Connie said. "If you were a man, I'd be tempted to kiss you."

Jill's brow furrowed in a frown. "That's pretty forward of her to spray you with perfume." Her shimmering black hair reached halfway down her back. Elegant in a pale pink cocktail sheath, she sent a flirty wave to her husband across the room before she returned her attention to Samantha. "Have you danced with Cole yet? He's been watching you all evening."

Samantha felt her face heat up. "So help me Jill, if you attempt any matchmaking this weekend…"

"I'll be good. Maybe." Jill smiled mischievously as she brought her champagne glass to her red lips.

"I like the perfume. I wonder what it's called," Connie said.

"She said it was a potion," Samantha said.

"A potion?" Jill's right brow lifted curiously.. "For what?"

Before she could reply, Connie handed her a champagne goblet. "Whatever it's called, I think it worked. Quick, drink this. We've got Romeo at 6 o'clock."

"Would you like to dance?" A deep male voice spoke over her shoulder.

Samantha turned to scrutinize the speaker. Gone was Cole's dinner jacket, and his white dress shirt lay open at the neck in sharp contrast to his tan. She wore kitten heels tonight and Cole towered over her, easily reaching six feet. His green eyes smiled warmly and she liked how his sandy-colored hair was cut in short layers, so tidy that a woman might be tempted to run her fingers through his hair …

Oh, dear. Samantha scrambled for an excuse to refuse the dance. What could she say? *"No thank you. You're extremely attractive and super nice but I'm sure there's something wrong with you."*

Now that she thought about it, both Connie and Jill had warned her against dating the men she'd met at those last two weddings. Tonight, however, they were working overtime trying to push her into Cole's arms. Did her friends know something she didn't?

Still . . . better safe than sorry—again. Darn these romantic weddings that kept her from seeing beyond first impressions. Hence, her new rule. *Never date a man you meet at a wedding.*

She realized Cole waited for an answer. "My friends and I were about ready to get a drink."

"I believe your friends have ditched you." His smile didn't quite hide his amusement.

Sure enough. Jill and Connie had disappeared like mist dissipating in the heat of a summer morning.. Samantha drained the glass of champagne.

Cole guided her to the dance floor with a hand lightly touching her lower back.

Under the twinkling lights with the night sky above, Cole swung her easily into his arms. Maybe this wasn't so dangerous, after all, as long as they just danced. She'd slip away like Cinderella the moment the song ended. Sounded easy enough. On a heady, champagne buzz, she smiled up into his handsome face.

Strong arms pulled her closer, against his muscular body. So close, she could feel the rhythm of his heart.

There was no gaining any space between them. His hand held firm at her lower back where material met bare skin. He expertly moved them to the slow beat of the music. His thighs brushed against the silky fabric of her dress. Her wedding-dating rule attempted to fight its way through the champagne affect to no avail.

She felt his breath against her temple. She caught a fragrantly heady whiff of whiskey.

He pulled back just enough to smile down at her. His teeth gleamed white against his tan skin in the dusk of the night. "So you're an old college friend of Margo's?"

"Yes, we all roomed together while attending UW, me, Margo, Jill and Connie."

"University of Washington?" he confirmed, with a lift of his eyebrow.

"Yes. And you went to Texas A&M?"

"You've been asking around?" he teased.

She felt her cheeks warm. Yes, she had. "Margo's grandmother is smitten with you," she teased back. "She had a lot to say about you."

"It tends to be the grandmothers who like me the best. I don't mind," he added. "They remind me of my grandmother who I miss."

She hardly believed it was only grandmothers who liked him best. How sweet that he favored their attention out of sentimental reasons. She didn't mind when he, once again, drew her closer.

It was Margo, calling out to the DJ to replay Etta James, saying that it was the 'most romantic song in the world', that broke through the champagne haze. The word 'romantic' causing the most alarm. The wedding-dating rule began to overpower the weakening effect of the champagne.

Realizing her predicament, Samantha searched for a safe topic. Her dance partner beat her to it.

"The four of you seem very close."

"We are. We stay in touch by phone or email and also have our regular GNO."

"What's that?" he asked.

"Girls' Night Out. Only we make it a long weekend, somewhere."

"Ah," he replied. "I do the same with my college buddies only we call it beer somewhere."

Once again, in spite of herself, she liked his sense of humor, easy smile, and the crow's feet at the corner of his eyes. They moved easily together on the dance floor, as though they were familiar with being in each other's arms. Samantha felt confused. Was it really a comfortable sense of familiarity spiced with the attraction she felt for him? Or was she under the influence of her romantic condition?

Her hand rested on his shoulder and she felt the heat of his skin through the expensive cotton. She bit down on her bottom lip, hoping that he couldn't feel how fast her heart raced.

His hand moved down her back to rest at the lowest possible place on her tailbone. Any further and he'd have a hand on her fanny. She considered, for a moment, stepping on his toe when she realized that there were fewer guests dancing beneath the stars at this late hour. Was it her imagination or had the lights dimmed? It would be crazy to suspect that Cole had anything to do with the seductive slowing of the evening. Or did Jill and Connie have a hand in this?

She realized too late that Cole had moved them closer to the edge of the dance floor. The expression in his eyes was unreadable. They slowly danced through the opening in a hedge to a private sitting area where a water fountain splashed and gurgled.

They were no longer dancing although the music continued beyond the tall hedge. They stood motionless beneath the stars. The silvery moon their only observer.

"I should go," Samantha whispered softly.

"Me, too."

Yet, neither made to leave.

Cole's hands lingered at her hips. A gentle tug brought her closer. Surely he felt her heart beating now? His fingers found their way to the rhinestone clip that secured her chignon and her hair tumbled free to whisper like silk across her shoulders. With a hand to the nape of her neck, he expertly tilted her face up to his. And he'd kissed her.

Chapter Two

The mid-morning sky had the makings of a beautiful, sunny day. Those who had volunteered to decorate for the wedding had gathered for breakfast at the home of the groom's parents. Lake Whatcom sparkled as if a thousand silver sequins lay just beneath its smooth surface. As the morning warmed toward the promised eighty-degree temperature, sparrows chirped and jumped from branch to branch in the lilac bushes, taking their morning shower from the dew off the foliage.

Although the weatherman warned of a possible summer storm rolling in, the energetic wedding planner dismissed the alert and assured the bride that the weather would be perfect. Rita had everything under control, or in her apron pockets. The wedding would go on, the champagne would flow and all would work out just splendidly. Or so they'd hoped.

A sweet breeze off the lake slipped right through the thin material of Samantha's sleeveless cotton top. A drop of condensation fell from the chilled glass she held in her hands. Absentmindedly, she wiped the water from her leg where bare skin met the hem of her white denim shorts. She'd yet to take a sip of the tomato juice concoction forced into her hands by the cheerful host who couldn't be convinced that not everyone had a champagne hangover.

Directly across from the Caruthers' home, a lush green island sat in the middle of Lake Whatcom. A canopy of green leafed maple trees covered its crown, interlaced with the red bark of madrona trees. To the south side of the island, the brownish color of the cliff was visible. The north side of the island sat at lake level with a sandy beach. Hours from now, the wedding would take place on the island. Would she be prepared to see Cole by then?

Slowly she placed her finger against her lips, still feeling his kiss from last night. She closed her eyes and felt again how his arms wrapped around her in a gentle and friendly manner. But the kiss clearly went over the line of 'friends only'. What exactly, had she expected in that ultra-secluded and shadowy balcony off the terrace? It was the perfect place for a kiss; leading her to believe that he'd planned how the night would go.

Was it unfair to blame this all on Cole? Should she give him the benefit of the doubt? Maybe he hadn't meant for it to happen, and had succumbed, like her, to a romantic evening, good whiskey, bubbly champagne, starry nights and all. Maybe Etta James was actually a hypnotist.

He'd kissed her, none-the-less; a kiss tasting of whiskey and the chocolate dessert. One that, even now, increased the beating of her heart.

"Samantha, what are you doing? We're waiting for you." Rita brought her back to reality as she beckoned from the top porch step of the grand lodge-style home where the bride would make-ready for her big day.

Inside, the house bustled with activity—filled with in-laws, aunts, uncles, and cousins. Some of whom had stayed in the guest rooms of the large 3,000 square foot home with Tuscany accents and gleaming wood floors. Others, like Samantha and her friends, had stayed in the town's hotels.

Earlier that morning, the spacious kitchen had held enough volunteer cooks to produce an over-loaded buffet-style breakfast. Platters had overflowed with waffles, crepes, sausage, eggs, hash browns, fruit, and gallons of steaming hot coffee. Samantha had shared breakfast at the large table, glad to be amongst the morning's bustle and confusion. It had been just the distraction she needed to keep from thinking about Cole.

Yet, here she was now, alone at the shoreline by the willow tree with its delicate branches gently swaying above the water that lapped to shore. She had to stop thinking about the feel of Cole's lips against hers and the slow, hypnotic way they had danced to the seductive rhythm and lyrics of *At Last*. The song had been meant for Margo and Rob, but Samantha had felt the world slow down as an intangible curtain of intimacy wrapped around her and Cole. She couldn't even recall when Margo and Rob left last night, or her friends. She only remembered the kiss.

"Samantha?" Rita called to her again. "Are you okay?"

"I'll be right there."

How was she going to get through this day, act as if nothing had happened, as if she didn't feel a thing? Was there a cure for a romantic at heart, one easily bewitched by a beautiful summer wedding and all its trimmings beneath canopies of lighted trees, candlelight, and fountains of champagne?

She looked down at the drink she held. Her host's idea of garnishment was a pickled pearl onion and small anchovy on a stick. Would it cure a kissing hangover as well?

Quickly, before she could talk herself out of trying the awful-looking drink, she put the onion and anchovy in her mouth and, without chewing, swallowed them whole as she drained the tomato juice concoction, spiked with hints of tabasco and lemon juice. Her eyes watered and a shiver ran down her spine. The day would tell what all that drink cured. If anything, it fortified her enough to smile at the cheery wedding planner as she joined her on the porch.

Rita beamed as if one of her own had returned home. "Well, there's my little helper. The supply boats are leaving now for the island." Rita stood barely five feet tall in her uniform of track shoes, jeans, and white polo shirt. Her red working apron was tied around her thick waist, ready for action. The pockets bulged with more items than her evening apron. Visible were notebooks, pens, tissue, hand sanitizer, tape measurer, first aid kit and a needle and thread kit. Rita also came armed with a clipboard. She tucked it under her arm, and, reaching up, put the palms of her hands on either side of Samantha's face.

"This is going to be a beautiful day full of love and good things." Rita looked puzzled for a moment. Her hands dropped to Samantha's shoulders and she gave her a little shake. "I should have used something stronger on you."

Samantha remembered too late the other items Rita kept in her apron pockets. From the depths came another small bottle only this one had a green cap. Before Samantha could jump out of range, she was sprayed from head to foot with some mystery potion.

"What now?" She could taste it on her lips. Quite quickly, her frustration with Rita dissipated as she breathed in the exotic scent of coconut and jasmine that transported her to a sun-drenched beach with balmy breezes and no cares in the world.

"That's my secret potion for those with an extreme case of 'romance is for the birds'."

"It's lovely," Samantha found herself saying.

Rita looked pleased as she pocketed her arsenal. "Unless you're even more stubborn than I think you are, that one should do the trick."

"Do the trick for what?" Samantha felt a river of euphoria moving lazily through her veins and blamed it on the tomato juice concoction.

"Never mind. Although there is something you shouldn't do for the next hour, only—darn, I can't remember what it is. Hold on a 'sec." Rita dug around in her apron and pulled out a packet of notecards rubber-banded together.   "There are special instructions to follow with that potion."

"Samantha! Come on. Let's go!" Connie waved to her from the dock.

"I'll see you later," Samantha said to Rita.

"Wait." Rita hastily shuffled through the notecards.

"It's alright. I'm good." Samantha set off across the side yard to the U-shaped dock that the Caruthers shared with their neighbors.

"There you are!" Jill greeted her excitedly, her hair pulled up in a ponytail. "You disappeared after breakfast."

"Went for a walk," Samantha said as she joined her friends.

"Well it must have done you good. You're looking very vibrant and cheerful. Or maybe it's something else that's put a smile on your face. Is he tall, tanned, and charming?"

Still feeling as if she were in a tropical paradise with no cares in the world, she made no reply, only smiled.

Wearing colorful T-shirts over their summer shorts, Jill and Connie stood beside a blue and white Malibu watercraft belonging to Rob's parents. Moored behind the sleek ski boat was another boat built for speed, a yellow and white Nautique on loan from one of the uncles who lived up the lake. Both boats were ready to go with a cargo of decorations, linens, and fresh flowers packed carefully in open boxes. Tucked in behind the boats was an inflatable dingy, tied to the dock and bobbing gently with the motion of the water.

"Mm. Now what scent are you wearing?" Connie sipped from a coffee cup, leaving a smear of pink lipstick. "I swear, I'm tempted to carry you off to an exotic island."

"Girl, you are a born comedian," Jill laughed.

The anchovy had left a fishy taste in Samantha's mouth. "Mind if I have a sip of your coffee?" she asked Connie.

"Sure. Go ahead and finish it."

She downed the lukewarm beverage, which did the trick of covering the taste of the fish. Normally a decaf drinker, she felt an immediate and unaccustomed rush from Connie's caffeinated coffee.

"Sammy," Connie nudged her arm, "don't look now, but your dance partner has arrived."

Two tall, broad shouldered men climbed from a black SUV, with garment bags hanging from the hooks above the rear passenger doors. Both men were grinning as they carried on what appeared to be an enjoyable discussion.

Cole was here.

The empty coffee cup dropped from her hands and rolled off the dock into the lake. Neither Jill nor Connie noticed; their attention only on the new arrivals.

What Samantha could only assume was a caffeine buzz annihilated the lazy day beach buzz. Cole's appearance this early must mean he'd come to help decorate.

"My God, Cole's in great shape for a forty-year old." Jill was happily married with three young boys but that didn't keep her from staring, unabashed. She shaded her eyes from the sun. "Who is that with him? I don't recall seeing him at the party last night."

The second man looked a few years younger with the same sandy-colored hair, only worn longer than Cole's thick, short layers. In plaid golf shorts and casual T-shirts with top-siders on their feet, they both sported golden tans.

"I think they're brothers," Connie said. "I overheard Cole telling Rob that his brother was flying in early this morning." She pulled a tube of lipstick from the pocket of her shorts. "Their family is in the boat building business," she said. "I think they build yachts or commercial fishing vessels, something like that."

"Which one is it?" Jill laughed.

"Sorry, can't remember the details. I was on my fourth glass of champagne by then. Damn, but the younger one is sure cute." She turned to Samantha. "Have you talked to Cole since last night?"

"No."

"No exchange of phone numbers?" Jill teased.

Samantha didn't reply. It would mean having to tell them about the kiss and what had happened after the kiss.

The two men headed toward the house, until Cole glanced in their direction. She caught her breath. It was the barest of movements, but Samantha thought he'd hesitated at whether to change direction. She blew a sigh of relief when they disappeared from view, obviously deciding to continue toward the house. Her relief quickly turned to disappointment at the thought that he'd given up so easily.

"Well, that's odd. Why didn't he join us? He certainly saw you," Jill said.

"Doesn't everyone need to report in to Rita?" Little butterflies danced in Samantha's stomach and her pulse beat overtime.

"By the way," Connie said with a smile, "where did you two go after the last dance?"

"Yes, do tell." Jill joined in with a grin.

"What?" Samantha said, pulling her cell phone from the pocket of her denim shorts and checking the time.

"Do we need to remind you? You and Cole were dancing. Actually, you started off dancing, but then you were all over each other. Next thing we knew, the two of you were nowhere to be seen."

"I don't remember any of that. Look, I don't know where he went, but I left." Samantha jumped into the boat. "Let's push off and get this load over to the island." She hurried forward to untie the bow mooring line, having to reach over the tarp-covered boxes in order to untie the line from the cleat on the dock.

"Hold on a sec'," Connie said. "You're not trying to avoid Cole, are you?"

"I don't know where you got that idea. Hurry up with that stern line, Jill."

"Don't we have to wait for someone to drive us?" Jill bent down to untie the line from the cleat.

"I've been on plenty of boats." Samantha didn't bother to coil up the rope, but dropped it onto the tarp. "Connie can vouch for me. I can drive this thing."

"If you're referring to last summer when you took our rented boat through the Montlake Cut on Lake Washington thinking the number on the buoy marker was the speed limit, well, I'm afraid—"

"Do you want to swim to the island?"

Connie took the hint and stepped gingerly into the boat looking for a place to sit. There wasn't much room for passengers with the seats and floor space filled with boxes of decorations.

"Look," Jill said, "either Cole's changed his mind about talking to you or Rita's given them no choice. Here they come now."

"Perfect!" Connie said. "They can ride over with us. Don't know where we'll put them, but I like cozy."

"They're not riding with us." The keys were in the ignition. Samantha started the engine. "Get in, Jill!" she said over the powerful inboard motor.

The noise didn't deter Connie from cross-examining her friend, raising her voice in order to be heard, "Why don't you want them to ride with us? Did something happen last night that you don't want to talk about?"

"Nothing happened," Samantha said. "I'm just not interested."

"You sure looked interested last night."

"Can we talk about something else?"

From the look on her face, Samantha knew that her friend wouldn't give up. Connie was no dummy. She'd figure it out sooner or later.

Samantha looked back to see that Jill struggled with untying the stern line.

"Wait a second," Connie said, "which one of my emails did you read last, April's love month or June's? Because your June horoscope for romance says that this is a good love month for your birth sign.

I bet you only read April. April's basically said to clean out your closets and get your oil changed."

Over her shoulder, Samantha saw the younger brother stop to assist Jill. He tossed the line onto the back of the boat.

Understanding dawned on Connie's face. Determined to avoid both Cole and a lecture on romance from her friend, Samantha put her hand to the throttle. Suddenly the boat rocked under the weight of a new arrival. Muscled arms went around her to shut off the engine and to push the throttle to neutral.

"You can't judge all men by the jerks you've met at past weddings," Connie's advice rang out over the all too sudden silence.

Cringing inwardly, she avoided meeting Cole's gaze from his spot beside her seat. Her gaze followed the direction he pointed, to the third mooring line securing the boat to the cleat within reach of the driver's seat. Embarrassment heated her face.

Cole leaped agilely back to the dock to untie the line. Without a word, he handed the rope to Samantha.

"Thanks," she said.

"You're welcome."

"You two are welcome to ride over with us." Connie, with her attention on more interesting things than Samantha's love life, moved over to the starboard side and held out her hand to the younger brother. "Hi, I'm Connie."

Samantha expected her to add her single status, age and how many nights a week she was available.

"Grant." The younger man smiled and shook Connie's hand.

"Hello, again," Jill said to Cole, ever the polite hostess wherever she went. "Remember us from last night?" She hesitated for a moment before a mischievous grin spread across her face. "You certainly must remember Samantha."

Good manners demanded she properly acknowledge Cole and she smiled as best she could. Her dance partner pulled his sunglasses over his eyes as he returned a smile equally as stiff as the one she'd given him.

"If the five of you wouldn't mind getting this first load over to the island, I'll love you forever." Rita race-walked toward them as she checked items off her clipboard. "We're expecting the two rented party barges to be delivered here any moment so when you return, tie up at the end of the dock if you would." She held the whistle in such a way that it looked like she was about ready to blow on it and say, "on your mark."

The boat lurched as Connie suddenly jumped onto the dock. She grabbed Grant by the elbow. "Let's take the other boat."

Jill was right on their heels. "Good idea."

Her careful plan to avoid Cole backfired with a casual wave from Jill. She realized that she was powerless up against any tactics her friends might employ with their matchmaking schemes. She thought back to how the two had thrown Margo, a single mother of twins, and Rob together. Nervously she wiped her palms across the seat of her shorts; first homemade love potions, now plotting friends. "In you go," Rita instructed Cole. "When you get over to the island, I'll need you two big, strong men to move any patio furniture off the terrace and over to the east side of the house." Rita bent down and whispered to Samantha. "I found the recipe card. Don't have any caffeine for a few hours. The potion won't work, then."

"How about you let me handle my own love life," Samantha shot back.

"Oh, but that's the problem I see, dear." Rita looked genuinely concerned. "You won't have one if you don't take a chance. That's where the potion helps." She stood and waved cheerfully at both boats. "Off you go, troops."

With ease and familiarity, Cole climbed back on board and pushed them away from the rubber-padded dock.

Samantha half expected this seasoned boatman to oust her from the driver's seat after her near serious mistake. Instead, he moved a box to make room on the passenger seat across from her.

"You got this?"

She nodded, pleased that he trusted her ability to pilot the craft.

Samantha turned the key, and with a careful look for any unseen lines attached to the dock, she turned the wheel gently and eased the craft forward. The stern safely cleared the dock. The boat behind them started up with Grant at the wheel.

As soon as they were clear of the 'no wake' zone, she increased their speed and headed toward the island. The wind cooled her face. Thankfully, the noise from the boat engine made small talk nearly impossible.

Although Cole looked relaxed, she could feel the tension between them. Dark glasses hid any expression in his eyes, but by the set of his jaw, there was certainly something on his mind. She had a feeling that this man wasn't accustomed to a woman pushing him away and running off into the night.

Chapter Three

At the island, they tied up at the dock where lake water lapped ashore across the smooth round rocks of the pebbled beach. The trailing branches of a large willow tree cascaded over the wide stone steps that butted up to the dock creating a green curtain to pass through as they followed the curving steps up the sloping hillside to the single-story house of glass and steel.

"What a gorgeous home," Jill exclaimed.

With the help from Cole and Grant, who each carried two to three boxes, they made quick work in unloading the boats, setting the decorations inside the house on the counters of the stainless steel kitchen.

To allow the cooling lake breeze into the home, they opened the Japanese-style sliding glass doors that stretched around three sides. The rear of the house was partially built into the rocky portion of the island and the windows in the bedrooms and bathrooms were set up high to receive any natural light.

"The view is breathtaking." Samantha stepped out onto the terrace.

"Not a bad place for a get-a-way," Cole commented as he joined her. "I can picture myself down there on the beach with a bon fire and no cares in the world other than whether my beer stayed cold or not."

With that icebreaker, the tension between them floated away in the warm breeze.

"S'mores," Samantha said. "A bon fire on the beach requires s'mores."

"Hot dog on a stick, burnt beyond recognition."

"Star gazing," she added.

"Definitely." He smiled at her.

"Hey, you two," Jill said from inside, "you can visit when the slow dancing starts again tonight."

Smiling, Cole went to help his brother move the patio furniture.

Back inside, and feeling her face flush warm, Samantha shook a warning finger at her friends. "He's not my type," she said.

Connie and Jill grinned at each other.

The wedding and celebration following would take place on the slate covered terrace that covered more square feet than the home. An outdoor fireplace stood at the far end of the terrace along a low rock wall that doubled as seating. A wedding arbor stood in front of the fireplace.

Either the island caretaker or their industrious wedding planner had set out colorful cushions along the wall. Folding chairs would be brought in for the guest before the ceremony.

From a box of wedding decorations, Grant pulled out a string of lights. "What are we supposed to do with these?"

"We're stringing them from post to post." Connie pointed to the terrace and the steel posts set along the rock wall, the posts doing dual duty as exterior lighting and supporting the hanging baskets of flowering annuals.

Connie took charge of the decorating. One group strung lights and garlands of fresh flowers on the terrace while another decorated the great room in the same manner. Climbing onto a stool from the breakfast bar, with Connie by her side holding an armful of roses, hydrangeas and tiny lights, Samantha began to tack up the garland across one of the open sliding doors.

"On second thought," Connie said, "it just doesn't look right having two guys hanging garland together." She called out through the open doors to Cole. "Trade places with me and don't ask questions."

Just like that, it happened. Samantha was once again at the mercy of her friend's matchmaking.

Cole now stood next to the stool dutifully holding the garland. "What was that all about?"

Samantha finished pushing a tack into the wall before she replied, "Connie thought two men shouldn't hang ribbons of garland together."

Cole laughed. "I agree. I'd much rather help you."

Stepping down from the stool proved to be a bit tricky holding tacks in one hand and garland in another.

"My shoulder is at your disposal," Cole said.

She eyed his strong frame and placed her hand on his shoulder. Even with his assistance, her dismount did not go smoothly. She mistook the distance to the floor and lost her balance.

He dropped the garland and a strong arm caught her to him. She'd let go of her end of the garland and her arm was now hooked around his neck.

A teasing light warmed his eyes. "Being this close only led to trouble last night."

She hastily released her grip on him and repositioned the stool under the next doorway.

"That's not what started the trouble," she said. "You should have a talk with your adventurous hands."

"My hands couldn't help themselves. You're a lovely woman."

Although his charm was working on her, she did her best to focus on her task. She proceeded to climb back on the stool, using the doorframe for support.

"Oh, I see. You prefer doorframes to men." He'd dutifully followed her and let out several yards of the garland as she began to pin another length over the doorway.

She smiled at his sense of humor. "They tend not to give a girl a hard time."

"I'm a pretty nice guy, just ask around."

"Just hand me the garland." She realized she truly enjoyed his easy manner.

"So you don't date men you meet at weddings all because of a few jerks?"

Samantha dropped a tack. "Don't believe everything Connie says."

"Is it true?" Cole stooped to retrieve the tack and handed it back to her. "Am I completely out of luck?"

She liked that he cared and had enough confidence to test his chances with her. Still, it wasn't enough to chance it. She couldn't let a romantic setting blind her again. She had to be careful that she didn't like his persistence too much. What if all there was to Cole was his good looks and charm?

"It was a long time ago." That was all she would say. As for his second question, she couldn't truthfully answer. She pushed the tack into the garland to secure it to the wall.

"Are you over them?"

"Absolutely!" she said and laughed as she arranged the garland to her liking. "I blame the romantic music and a starry night on my poor choice in boyfriends."

Cole remained silent and Samantha debated whether to borrow his shoulder again.

"We could go back in time and I could fly up here and run into you at the gas station." There was a teasing light in his eye. "Unless you feel a gas station is too romantic of a setting."

Samantha used the doorframe to step safely off the stool. "Cole, you live in California. It wouldn't work." They would need more garland to cover the next set of windows. Searching for another box of decorations was her excuse to look away from him.

"You know," Cole began, "I wasn't asking you to marry me, just working up towards a cup of coffee somewhere."

"Who's getting married?" Grant said as the work party came in off the terrace.

"Smooth move," Connie mouthed to her with an irritated frown between her eyes.

A cell phone rang saving Samantha from the uncomfortable silence.

She dug her cell phone from her pocket and recognized Margo's caller ID.

"How's the bride?" she said.

"By any chance are the twins with you?"

"No."

"No one's seen them since breakfast," Margo's voice was shaky.

"Hold on. Let me ask the others." Samantha turned to the group. "Any of you see the twins, Wilson and Orlando, since breakfast?"

They all shook their heads.

Samantha spoke calmly to Margo. "It's a big house, have you looked in all the rooms?"

"We've looked everywhere and we've been searching for the last twenty minutes."

Cole stood before Samantha. "May I talk to her?"

She handed him the phone.

Cole walked away a few paces and spoke to Margo in a calm, sure voice.

"Cole's good at this," Grant said. "He's been involved with search and rescue for years down in California and has even volunteered as a first responder during natural disasters, part of his training from the Marines."

They'd formed a close circle as they waited for Cole to finish his call.

"They're probably just playing hike and seek." Connie rubbed her bare shoulders as she chewed on her bottom lip.

Cole's conversation lasted only a few minutes. He returned the phone to Samantha. A worried frown creased his brow.

"I'm taking one of the boats back. Grant, let's go. The inflatable dingy is missing."

"Oh, no." Connie's shaking hand flew to her mouth.

"Could they even manage the dingy?" Samantha said. "They're only eight years old."

"You don't know boys," said Jill.

"I'm going with you," said Connie, hurrying after Cole.

"Me, too." Samantha was right behind her.

"I'll stay here in case they show up," said Jill.

On the dock, Samantha raced ahead to untie the forward lines on the Malibu. Connie was already in the Nautique, skippered by Grant.

"I take it you're with me." Cole deftly untied the mooring line and walked onto the boat by way of the stern.

She nodded.

"Good. Keep a look out for the yellow dingy," Cole instructed as he started the boat. "Let's keep our fingers crossed that this will end well."

In the distance, thunder rolled above the foothills.

"Hang on," Cole said.

Unable to relax, Samantha did not take a seat but instead stood next to Cole at the helm.

The boat sped across the lake with the wind in her face and tugging on her long hair. This day wasn't supposed to turn out like this. This was Margo's day, a day of happiness and a chance for her to once again have a family.

A warm hand momentarily covered hers where she gripped the windshield. She knew his touch was meant to give hope and encouragement. Nonetheless, fear for the twins gripped her heart.

On the hood of his SUV, Cole spread out an area map and began coordinating the teams of volunteers who had gathered. Several neighbors had been called in to search the shoreline with their boats.

A vehicle came screeching around the corner at the top of the driveway. They watched as Rob's jeep approached, non-too-slowly.

Samantha stood with her arm around Margo after convincing her to change from her spa robe into jeans and top and to put shoes on her bare feet. The outfit change was done in the open garage while Margo's mother held up a beach towel. Margo refused to go back into the house until her boys were safe. The frantic and teary mother broke free and ran into Rob's arms the moment he stepped from the vehicle.

Although the sheriff's department was on their way, the volunteers assembled were ready to move out.

"Everyone, listen up." Cole stood on the running board of his vehicle. "The boys are wearing matching Seahawk jerseys and denim shorts." He glanced at Margo who wiped her eyes. He faced the search party again. "Does every team have a cell phone? Each team should also have the blankets, food and water my aunt and uncle put together should your team find two tired and hungry little boys. Also, don't forget warm jackets. Chances are we're going to get rained on."

The parents of the bride and groom, along with Margo's grandmother, remained behind should the boys return to the house. The search parties consisting of relatives, friends and neighbors set out. Several groups took to the wooded hillside across the road and several vehicles began driving slowly in each direction along the lake road. Those on foot went door-to-door.

Boats spanned the water. Margo and Rob joined Grant and Connie in the Nautique to head south while Cole, Samantha, Rita and a neighbor set off in the Malibu to search the northern shoreline. The twin's names were called out, repeatedly, across the water, echoing off the wooded hillside.

In the bow of the Malibu, Rita held a pair of binoculars to her eyes. The neighbor, an elderly gentleman still in his golf clothes and windbreaker from an early morning tee-time, sat on the bench seat at the stern scanning the shoreline.

Samantha was again standing at the helm next to Cole.

"Do you have kids?" Cole asked as he maintained a moderate speed, his eyes intently searching the water ahead and to either side.

"No. Do you?" Her hands felt like ice, her insides a knot of fear that they'd find an empty dingy drifting on the lake.

Cole shook his head in reply.

Rain began to fall. Beads of water ran down the windshield. Samantha shivered as a sudden wind picked up.

"Put this on." Cole pulled a gray fleece jacket from a duffel bag at his feet. "Don't mind the dog hair."

She slid her arms into the soft fleece that held the faint scent of Cole's cologne and, sure enough, several strands of course, black dog hair clung to the jacket that immediately began to warm her.

She placed a hand on Cole's arm. "Did anyone look to see if their life jackets were gone?"

"I looked," he said. "They're still in the garage."

Samantha's heart sank. She couldn't even focus on working the zipper up on the fleece jacket.

"Take the wheel," Cole said.

She did so and he zipped up the fleece coat for her.

She smiled her thanks and the warmth in his eyes offered reassurance once again.

Cole held his cell phone in one hand watching for a text message or incoming call. Suddenly his phone lit up.

He cut back on the engine as he answered. He listened for a moment. "Got it. We're on our way." He pocketed the phone. "Rob just took a call from Jill. She's spotted an inflatable dingy on shore on the far side of the island. No sign of the twins but we're that much closer to finding them." He banked the boat hard to starboard and they changed course. "Hang on, everyone."

He put the throttle forward and they sped toward the island, bouncing over the waves kicked up by the incoming storm. The Nautique could be seen further up the lake making a sweeping turn toward the island.

"The water's getting choppier," Cole said. "We're going to get wet."

Samantha shielded her face from the spray coming over the bow and blowing in sideways as they sped along.

"We'll find them! I know we will!" Rita shouted from her seat in the bow, giving everyone a thumbs-up as the wind whipped her hair around her face and thunder rumbled overhead. "We have a wedding in three hours and counting. Come Hell or high—"

A sheet of water came over the bow to drench the wedding planner.

Chapter Four

The Nautique was tied to the dock and its occupants racing up the stone steps to the house as they approached the dock. Cole grabbed hold of the cleat and held the boat against the dock while Rita and the older neighbor climbed out.

Grant returned at a fast jog down the steps. "Jill found one of the twin's water wings at the top of the trail, about ten feet from the edge of the cliff."

"Oh, no!" Rita exclaimed.

Cole shoved off. "We'll go around to the south side. "Grant, you and Rob take the trail."

The powerful ski boat sped along the shoreline toward the cliff. As Cole guided the boat around, the steep wall of rock rose up above them. Samantha shielded her eyes against the rain to search for any sign of the twins. She didn't see anything but wet, black rock with tree roots and weeds growing in niches.

Cole pulled back on the throttle and they motored in slowly for a closer look. The backside of the island was sheltered from the wind from the north and lay in shadows. The water was quieter and looked shimmering dark, the color of molten steel with only the ripples from the boat and the rain drops disturbing its surface.

With one hand on the wheel, Cole was on his feet standing beside her, so close that their arms brushed as they intently searched the shoreline and the rock wall.

"I can't imagine what Margo is going through," Samantha said softly, shivering even in the soft fleece of the jacket. Goosebumps prickled along her bare legs.

Rainwater ran down the sides of his face. Cole cupped his hands around his mouth, "Orlando! Wilson!"

Suddenly she saw movement near the top of the cliff. "There!" She pointed.

Light reflected off the silver stripes on the boy's jerseys. Grant's head appeared at the top of the rock wall. He motioned with his arms, crisscrossing over his head before pointing straight down. He'd seen the twins as well.

The boys were ten feet down from the top, huddled together on a ledge.

"How do we get to them?" Samantha said.

"Not sure yet."

They motored cautiously toward shore. Cole wiped beads of rain off the face of the depth finder several times as they approached the shallows. When the depth finder read ten feet, he cut the engine. Looking over the side, Samantha could see the sandy bottom.

Cole's cell phone rang. He quickly answered, "Yeah, Grant. What does it look like from up there?" He listened briefly before replying, "We can't waste any time then, let's do this."

"What is it? What's wrong?" Samantha said.

"Typically in a situation like this, we'd wait for ropes and harnesses. From what Grant can see, the boys are barely hanging on, they're cold and growing tired." As he'd talked, Cole moved forward to open the compartments beneath the seat in the bow. Within minutes, he'd secured the long rope of the anchor to the boat before tossing the small anchor over the bow. "The good news is that the rock wall isn't as sheer as it looks from down here. Grant says it has a grade so it shouldn't be too difficult getting the twins down."

He was back at her side, eying the slope over the top of her head. "I'm not sure how long this will take."

There was only a foot of space between them when he reached for the hem of his shirt. Her only warning that the shirt was coming off was the initial sight of his belly button and the dark hairline that traveled down to the top of his shorts. A moment later, she was staring at hard packed abs and powerful shoulder muscles.

"Hang onto these for me."

Into her cupped hands went the contents of his pockets: cell phone, wallet and a set of car keys attached to a key fob in the shape of a Labrador. The last she saw of Cole as he dove overboard was the white undersides of his bare feet.

"Be careful!" she called out when his sleek head broke the surface and he struck out towards shore in a powerful over-arm stroke.

The rain eased up making visibility easier as she watched the rescue. It was a harrowing twenty minutes as Cole slowly found handholds and toeholds as he scaled the rocky incline. From above, Grant worked his way down.

It wasn't until both Grant and Cole, each with a twin clinging tightly to their strong backs, had set foot on the beach that Samantha sank to the floor of the boat. The rain suddenly stopped, the dark clouds moved on and sunlight warmed the top of her head. She had watched Cole's progress so intently that her tight grip on his car keys left an imprint in the palm of her hand.

"Splendid!" Rita beamed and clapped her hands together as the newly married couple, still hanging onto the twins as they'd done throughout the ceremony, took to the dance floor as a pink and tangerine sky silhouetted the foothills. "I knew this would all work out, just splendidly."

Not all the decorations were up, as they'd run out of time, but the twinkling stars above added nature's magical touch. The terrace looked beautiful with long tails of white ribbons fluttering gently in the breeze and bouquets of flowers and strings of lights between the poles. Music played from the speakers tucked behind flower planters.

"Hand me that bottle of champagne." Connie appeared at her elbow. Already a little tipsy, she leaned against Samantha's shoulder with a starry look in her eye. "This evening couldn't be more romantic."

Samantha held her yellow chiffon bridesmaid gown out of the way and reached into the tub of melting ice that held champagne and beer.

She handed the dripping wet bottle to her friend. "I take it this isn't for you and me."

Connie grinned. "You've got your own Romeo."

Samantha had lost sight of Cole on the crowded terrace shortly following the nuptials. "I haven't seen him for the last half hour."

"Honey," Connie's speech slurred, but her romance advice was still up and running, "there comes a point when you have to let the man know that you're interested. Quit running hot and cold, my sweet little chicken shit." She placed a manicured finger under Samantha's chin, forcing her to make eye contact. "Do you like this guy?"

Samantha didn't have to think hard on that question. "Yes."

"Then take a chance. Remember, our mistakes are behind us."

For a fleeting moment, she caught a glimpse of Connie's past heartache flickering in her eyes.

"You and I are both older and wiser now, Sam— maybe not terribly older, or terribly wiser," she said, giving her a grin. "But, either way, we can never give up on someday finding the real thing." The ice-cold champagne bottle pressed against Samantha's bare arm as Connie leaned forward to kiss her on the forehead before she disappeared into the crowd.

The warm night breeze teased the chiffon layers of Samantha's gown. Several steps down on the terrace, couples danced slowly under the stars to the sexy voice of Frank Sinatra.

It had to be you, it had to be you...

I wandered around, and finally found the somebody who…

"They've got the right idea." Cole's voice, sexy and deep, came to her from behind.

She turned slowly, seeing him leaning against the lamp post behind her, strikingly handsome in a black tuxedo and white dress shirt minus the bow tie.

Samantha took a deep breath. *Steady girl.*

His gaze made a leisurely trail from her ankles to neckline; caressing her from her feet covered by strappy silver sandals to the single shoulder bared by her chiffon draped, figure hugging dress.

"This isn't exactly the best place to say this," Cole began, as guests moved between them, either to the dance floor or the house, "but I've been thinking about that kiss last night."

Samantha barely noticed the elbow in her side as a guest squeezed past. "You don't give up, do you?" *Thank goodness.*

"Not on a good thing I don't." His eyes locked on hers. Her pulse quickened. "There's also the fact that you're not avoiding me," he continued. "Not that very many women do avoid me." He grinned as he took a pull from his beer.

Samantha rolled her eyes, but smiled.

"What are we going to do about our problem?" he asked.

"I didn't notice we had a problem."

"Oh, we certainly do." He straightened from the post and closed the distance between them. "You want me to ask you out, but there's this distance thing I'm not so crazy about."

Samantha laughed. "Oh, you're very funny."

Cole tucked a strand of blond hair behind her ear. "Seattle is just so damn far away, I'm not sure it would work. Not even for a harmless cup of coffee."

Plain and simple, she liked this man. She didn't need Connie to hit her over the head to see that there was more to Cole than what had prompted Margo's grandmother to wave a fan across her face. Besides, she liked what his smile did to her pulse.

Out of the corner of her eye, she saw Rita threading her way through the crowd. She caught a glimpse of a small bottle in her hand. This one had a gold cap. In that instant, she decided Connie was right. She needed to take a chance. Her instincts told her that Cole was worth it. She could do this, and she didn't need the assistance of any potion.

Samantha locked her gaze onto Cole. "Grab a bottle of champagne and meet me at the boat."

She met the potion-maker on the terrace. Rita lifted her hand, no doubt ready to give her a liberal spritz of whatever the bottle held. Samantha restrained the woman's arm. "Stand down, lady. I've got this." The two exchanged knowing looks as Cole approached, carrying a bottle of champagne and two plastic champagne flutes.

Samantha spared a backward glance at him as they left the crowded terrace.

He caught up to her as she stepped through the willow tree's branches adorned with yards of gauzy white material to create a curtained entrance to the party. They stood alone on the dock, surrounded by the muted sounds of the wedding celebration. The night added its own music with the distant chirping of crickets and the lake water lapping at the shore beneath the dock. A gentle breeze stirred the filmy curtains to billow around them, creating an intimate cocoon. Once again, they were alone with only a silvery moon overhead.

Cole set down the champagne and glasses and gave her his full attention. She took a fistful of his shirt, drawing him against her. "I'm glad you don't give up so easily."

"Should we talk about this distance thing?" His arms circled around her.

"There's something you need to do first."

He smiled. "What would that be?"

"Remind me how that kiss went."

He pulled her tighter against his lean body with one arm, his thumb sensually stroking her lower back through the silky material of her dress. His eyes burned with passion, making her heart beat overtime. She barely felt his other hand at the nape of her neck before her hair tumbled to her bare shoulders.

She laughed, giving her head a shake. "Do you have something against up-do's?"

Sent her a brilliant smile. "Only when it comes to your hair. It's far too gorgeous to be pinned up." Cole zeroed in on her mouth, a man on a mission. Warm lips covered hers, gently at first, as if to taste for the first time. He slid his hands along her hips to the curve of her lower back. Heat from him intensified as did the depth of his kiss. She lifted to her toes, wrapping her arms around his neck. His strong hands cupped her bottom and lifted her off the ground.

He broke the kiss, breathing hard, his voice husky with emotion. "I'm thinking we should move to the boat."

She gave him an enthusiastic nod and slipped out of her heels as Cole jumped into the Malibu. She handed him the champagne and flutes and he placed them on a seat of the boat. He turned back to her and she stepped into his waiting arms. He swung her in beside him. They untied the mooring lines and Cole started up the boat. They motored a short distance away before Cole cut the engine. Back on the island, lights from the terrace twinkled through the trees as the subtle tones of the reception music floated out to them.

Cole stripped off his jacket and shoes then rolled up the sleeves of his dress shirt, revealing his tanned, strong forearms. In one movement, he lowered himself to the bench seat and pulled her onto his lap. "Now where were we?"

Samantha ran her hands along his arms, feeling the heat of his bare skin.

"I think you were kissing me," she said.

One moment they were sitting and the next they were stretched out on the bench seat and he'd pulled her beneath him. The skirt of her evening gown hiked up over her bare legs, trailing to the floor. "I think you'll be warmer this way." He scorched her with his smile.

Samantha indulged herself by running her fingers through the silky short layers of his hair. "You are so considerate."

"I can be more considerate." He smiled.

"How is that?"

"Your lips look cold." He kissed her again.

The warmth from his body covered hers, and she groaned with pleasure at how well they fit together. "I have a feeling we're going to be able to work out our problem."

"I think so, too." He brushed her hair from her eyes.

"It appears we've skipped the harmless cup of coffee," she teased.

His low chuckle surrounded them. "I was trying to be a proper gentleman but sometimes you have to go with your instincts."

"Mm, I agree." She gave him another kiss, and prepared herself to follow her own instincts. There, under the curtain of twinkling stars, with gentle waves lapping at the sides of the boat, something told her tonight was the start of a whole new life . . . for both of them.

ABOUT THE AUTHOR

Photo by Rachel Whitney

Carmine Valentine resides in the Seattle area. Writer of romantic suspense and paranormal, *Once Upon a Summer's Kiss* is her third published short romance. She is currently working on completing a romantic suspense novel titled *Killer Regrets* that is set in the San Juan Islands of Washington State.

Please visit her website at www.carminevalentine.com to keep abreast of what's coming next.

DEDICATION

To my GNO compadres: Denise Anderson, Lesli Mataya, Judy Robb and Diane Sherwood-Palmer

www.ingramcontent.com/pod-product-compliance
Lightning Source LLC
Chambersburg PA
CBHW071458170626
46811CB00007B/2619